BY E. LOCKHART

Family of Liars

We Were Liars

Genuine Fraud

Again Again

Fly on the Wall

Dramarama

The Disreputable History of Frankie Landau-Banks

THE RUBY OLIVER QUARTET

The Boyfriend List

The Boy Book

The Treasure Map of Boys

Real Live Boyfriends

The more you sweat in practice,
the less you bleed in battle,

#genuinefraud

GENUINE FRAUD

e. lockhart

xo E. lockhart

EMBER

Text copyright © 2017 by E. Lockhart
Cover photography copyright © 2019 by Getty Images/Jonathan Knowles

Visit us on the Web! GetUnderlined.com

Educators and librarians, for a variety of teaching tools,
visit us at RHTeachersLibrarians.com

The Library of Congress has cataloged the hardcover edition of this work as follows:
Names: Lockhart, E., author.
Title: Genuine fraud / E. Lockhart.
Description: Trade hardcover edition. | New York : Delacorte Press, 2017. |
Summary: Told through flashbacks, best friends Jule and Imogen are orphaned outcasts who will do almost anything to attain a happy, wealthy life
Identifiers: LCCN 2017023586 (print) | LCCN 2017036668 (ebook) |
ISBN 978-0-385-74477-5 (trade hardcover) | ISBN 978-0-385-39138-2 (ebook) |
ISBN 978-0-375-99184-4 (library binding) | ISBN 978-1-5247-7067-9 (export edition)
Subjects: | CYAC: Best friends—Fiction. | Friendship—Fiction. | Deception—Fiction. |
Impersonation—Fiction. | Orphans—Fiction. | Mystery and detective stories.
Classification: LCC PZ7.L79757 (ebook) | LCC PZ7.L79757 Gen 2017 (print) |
DDC [Fic]—dc23

ISBN 978-0-593-56717-3 (tr. pbk.)

Printed in the United States of America
10 9 8 7 6 5 4 3 2 1
2022 Ember Edition

Random House Children's Books supports the First Amendment
and celebrates the right to read.

For anyone who has been taught that *good* equals small and silent, here is my heart with all its ugly tangles and splendid fury.

Begin here:

📅 **THIRD WEEK IN JUNE, 2017**
📍 **CABO SAN LUCAS, MEXICO**

It was a bloody great hotel.

The minibar in Jule's room stocked potato chips and four different chocolate bars. The bathtub had bubble jets. There was an endless supply of fat towels and liquid gardenia soap. In the lobby, an elderly gentleman played Gershwin on a grand piano at four each afternoon. You could get hot clay skin treatments, if you didn't mind strangers touching you. Jule's skin smelled like chlorine all day.

The Playa Grande Resort in Baja had white curtains, white tile, white carpets, and explosions of lush white flowers. The staff members were nurselike in their white cotton garments. Jule had been alone at the hotel for nearly four weeks now. She was eighteen years old.

This morning, she was running in the Playa Grande gym. She wore custom sea-green shoes with navy laces. She ran without music. She had been doing intervals for nearly an hour when a woman stepped onto the treadmill next to hers.

This woman was younger than thirty. Her black hair was

in a tight ponytail, slicked with hair spray. She had big arms and a solid torso, light brown skin, and a dusting of powdery blush on her cheeks. Her shoes were down at the heels and spattered with old mud.

No one else was in the gym.

Jule slowed to a walk, figuring to leave in a minute. She liked privacy, and she was pretty much done, anyway.

"You training?" the woman asked. She gestured at Jule's digital readout. "Like, for a marathon or something?" The accent was Mexican American. She was probably a New Yorker raised in a Spanish-speaking neighborhood.

"I ran track in secondary school. That's all." Jule's own speech was clipped, what the British call BBC English.

The woman gave her a penetrating look. "I like your accent," she said. "Where you from?"

"London. St. John's Wood."

"New York." The woman pointed to herself.

Jule stepped off the treadmill to stretch her quads.

"I'm here alone," the woman confided after a moment. "Got in last night. I booked this hotel at the last minute. You been here long?"

"It's never long enough," said Jule, "at a place like this."

"So what do you recommend? At the Playa Grande?"

Jule didn't often talk to other hotel guests, but she saw no harm in answering. "Go on the snorkel tour," she said. "I saw a bloody huge moray eel."

"No kidding. An eel?"

"The guide tempted it with fish guts he had in a plastic milk jug. The eel swam out from the rocks. It must have been eight feet long. Bright green."

The woman shivered. "I don't like eels."

"You could skip it. If you scare easy."

The woman laughed. "How's the food? I didn't eat yet."

"Get the chocolate cake."

"For breakfast?"

"Oh, yeah. They'll bring it to you special, if you ask."

"Good to know. You traveling alone?"

"Listen, I'm gonna jet," said Jule, feeling the conversation had turned personal. "Cheerio." She headed for the door.

"My dad's crazy sick," the woman said, talking to Jule's back. "I've been looking after him for a long time."

A stab of sympathy. Jule stopped and turned.

"Every morning and every night after work, I'm with him," the woman went on. "Now he's finally stable, and I wanted to get away so badly I didn't think about the price tag. I'm blowing a lot of cash here I shouldn't blow."

"What's your father got?"

"MS," said the woman. "Multiple sclerosis? And dementia. He used to be the head of our family. Very macho. Strong in all his opinions. Now he's a twisted body in a bed. He doesn't even know where he is half the time. He's, like, asking me if I'm the waitress."

"Damn."

"I'm scared I'm gonna lose him and I hate being with him, both at the same time. And when he's dead and I'm an orphan, I know I'm going to be sorry I took this trip away from him, d'you know?" The woman stopped running and put her feet on either side of the treadmill. She wiped her eyes with the back of her hand. "Sorry. Too much information."

"S'okay."

"You go on. Go shower or whatever. Maybe I'll see you around later."

The woman pushed up the arms of her long-sleeved shirt and turned to the digital readout of her treadmill. A scar wound down her right forearm, jagged, like from a knife, not clean like from an operation. There was a story there.

"Listen, do you like to play trivia?" Jule asked, against her better judgment.

A smile. White but crooked teeth. "I'm excellent at trivia, actually."

"They run it every other night in the lounge downstairs," said Jule. "It's pretty much rubbish. You wanna go?"

"What kind of rubbish?"

"Good rubbish. Silly and loud."

"Okay. Yeah, all right."

"Good," said Jule. "We'll kill it. You'll be glad you took a vacation. I'm strong on superheroes, spy movies, YouTubers, fitness, money, makeup, and Victorian writers. What about you?"

"Victorian writers? Like Dickens?"

"Yeah, whatever." Jule felt her face flush. It suddenly seemed an odd set of things to be interested in.

"I love Dickens."

"Get out."

"I do." The woman smiled again. "I'm good on Dickens, cooking, current events, politics . . . let's see, oh, and cats."

"All right, then," said Jule. "It starts at eight o'clock in that lounge off the main lobby. The bar with sofas."

"Eight o'clock. You're on." The woman walked over and extended her hand. "What's your name again? I'm Noa."

Jule shook it. "I didn't tell you my name," she said. "But it's Imogen."

Jule West Williams was nice-enough-looking. She hardly ever got labeled *ugly,* nor was she commonly labeled *hot.* She was short, only five foot one, and carried herself with an uptilted chin. Her hair was in a gamine cut, streaked blond in a salon and currently showing dark roots. Green eyes, white skin, light freckles. In most of her clothes, you couldn't see the strength of her frame. Jule had muscles that puffed off her bones in powerful arcs—like she'd been drawn by a comic-book artist, especially in the legs. There was a hard panel of abdominal muscle under a layer of fat in her midsection. She liked to eat meat and salt and chocolate and grease.

Jule believed that the more you sweat in practice, the less you bleed in battle.

She believed that the best way to avoid having your heart broken was to pretend you don't have one.

She believed that the *way* you speak is often more important than anything you have to say.

She also believed in action movies, weight training, the power of makeup, memorization, equal rights, and the idea that YouTube videos can teach you a million things you won't learn in college.

If she trusted you, Jule would tell you she went to Stanford for a year on a track-and-field scholarship. "I got recruited," she explained to people she liked. "Stanford is Division One. The school gave me money for tuition, books, all that."

What happened?

Jule might shrug. "I wanted to study Victorian literature

and sociology, but the head coach was a perv," she'd say. "Touching all the girls. When he got around to me, I kicked him where it counts and told everybody who would listen. Professors, students, the *Stanford Daily*. I shouted it to the top of the stupid ivory tower, but you know what happens to athletes who tell tales on their coaches."

She'd twist her fingers together and lower her eyes. "The other girls on the team denied it," she'd say. "They said I was lying and that pervert never touched anybody. They didn't want their parents to know, and they were afraid they'd lose their scholarships. That's how the story ended. The coach kept his job. I quit the team. That meant I didn't get my financial aid. And that's how you make a dropout of a straight-A student."

After the gym, Jule swam a mile in the Playa Grande pool and spent the rest of the morning as she often did, sitting in the business lounge, watching Spanish instruction videos. She was still in her bathing suit, but she wore her sea-green running shoes. She'd put on hot pink lipstick and some silver eyeliner. The suit was a gunmetal one-piece with a hoop at the chest and a deep plunge. It was a very Marvel Universe look.

The lounge was air-conditioned. No one else was ever in there. Jule put her feet up and wore headphones and drank Diet Coke.

After two hours of Spanish she ate a Snickers bar for lunch and watched music videos. She danced around on her caffeine jag, singing to the line of swivel chairs in the empty lounge. Life was bloody gorgeous today. She liked that sad woman running away from her sick father, the woman with the interesting scar and the surprising taste in books.

They would kill it at trivia.

Jule drank another Diet Coke. She checked her makeup and kickboxed her own image in the reflective glass of the lounge window. Then she laughed aloud, because she looked both foolish and awesome. All the while, the beat pulsed in her ears.

The poolside bartender, Donovan, was a local guy. He was big-boned but soft. Slick hair. Given to winking at the clientele. He spoke English with the accent particular to Baja and knew Jule's drink: a Diet Coke with a shot of vanilla syrup.

Some afternoons, Donovan asked Jule about growing up in London. Jule practiced her Spanish. They'd watch movies on the screen above the bar as they talked.

Today, at three in the afternoon, Jule perched on the corner stool, still wearing her swimsuit. Donovan wore a Playa Grande white blazer and T-shirt. Stubble was growing on the back of his neck. "What's the movie?" she asked him, looking up at the TV.

"*Hulk.*"

"Which Hulk?"

"I don't know."

"You put the DVD in. How can you not know?"

"I don't even know there's two Hulks."

"There's three Hulks. Wait, I take that back. Multiple Hulks. If you count TV, cartoons, all that."

"I don't know which Hulk it is, Ms. Williams."

The movie went on for a bit. Donovan rinsed glasses and wiped the counter. He made a scotch and soda for a woman who took it off to the other end of the pool area.

"It's the second-best Hulk," said Jule, when she had his attention again. "What's the word for *Scotch* in Spanish?"

"*Escocés.*"

"*Escocés.* What's a good kind to get?"

"You never drink."

"But if I did."

"Macallan," Donovan said, shrugging. "You want me to pour you a sample?"

He filled five shot glasses with different brands of high-end Scotch. He explained about Scotches and whiskeys and why you'd order one and not the other. Jule tasted each but didn't drink much.

"This one smells like armpit," she told him.

"You're crazy."

"And this one smells like lighter fluid."

He bent over the glass to smell it. "Maybe."

She pointed to the third. "Dog piss, like from a really angry dog."

Donovan laughed. "What do the others smell like?" he asked.

"Dried blood," Jule said. "And that powder you use to clean bathrooms. Cleaning powder."

"Which one d'you like the best?"

"The dried blood," she said, sticking her finger in the glass and tasting it again. "Tell me what it's called."

"That's the Macallan." Donovan cleared the glasses. "Oh, and I forgot to say: a woman was asking about you earlier. Or maybe not you. She might have been confused."

"What woman?"

"A Mexican lady. Speaking Spanish. She asked about a white American girl with short blond hair, traveling alone," said Donovan. "She said freckles." He touched his face. "Across the nose."

"What did you tell her?"

"I said it's a big resort. Lots of Americans. I don't know who's staying alone and who's not."

"I'm not American," said Jule.

"I know. So I told her I hadn't seen anyone like that."

"That's what you said?"

"Yeah."

"But you still thought of me."

He looked at Jule for a long minute. "I did think of you," he said finally. "I'm not stupid, Ms. Williams."

Noa knew she was American.

That meant Noa was a cop. Or something. Had to be.

She had set Jule up, with all that talk. The ailing father, Dickens, becoming an orphan. Noa had known exactly what to say. She had laid that bait out—"my father is crazy sick"—and Jule had snapped it up, hungry.

Jule's face felt hot. She'd been lonely and weak and just bloody stupid, to fall for Noa's lines. It was all a ruse, so Jule would see Noa as a confidante, not an adversary.

Jule walked back to her room, looking as relaxed as she could. Once inside, she grabbed her valuables from the safe. She put on jeans, boots, and a T-shirt and threw as many clothes as would fit into her smallest suitcase. The rest she left behind. On the bed, she laid a hundred-dollar tip for Gloria, the maid she sometimes talked to. Then she wheeled the suitcase down the hall and tucked it next to the ice machine.

Back at the poolside bar, Jule told Donovan where the case was. She pushed a US twenty-dollar bill across the counter.

Asked a favor.

She pushed another twenty across and gave instructions.

In the staff parking lot, Jule looked around and found the bartender's little blue sedan, unlocked. She got in and lay down on the floor in the back. It was littered with empty plastic bags and coffee cups.

She had an hour to wait before Donovan finished his bar shift. With luck, Noa wouldn't realize anything was amiss until Jule was seriously late for trivia night, maybe around eight-thirty. Then she'd investigate the airport shuttle and the cab company records before thinking of the staff lot.

It was airless and hot in the car. Jule listened for footsteps.

Her shoulder cramped. She was thirsty.

Donovan would help her, right?

He would. He had already covered for her. He'd told Noa he didn't know anyone like that. He warned Jule and promised to collect the suitcase and give her a ride. She had paid him, too.

Besides, Donovan and Jule were friends.

Jule stretched her knees straight, one at a time, then folded herself back up in the space behind the seats.

She thought about what she was wearing, then took off her earrings and her jade ring, shoving them into her jeans pocket. She forced herself to calm her breathing.

Finally, there was the sound of a suitcase on rollers. The slam of the trunk. Donovan slipped behind the wheel, started the car, and pulled out of the lot. Jule stayed on the floor as he drove. The road had few streetlights. There was Mexican pop on the radio.

"Where d'you want to go?" Donovan asked eventually.

"Anywhere in town."

"I'm going home, then." His voice sounded predatory all of a sudden.

Damn. Was she wrong to have gotten in his car? Was Donovan one of those guys who thinks a girl who wants a favor has to mess around with him?

"Drop me a ways from where you live," she told him sharply. "I'll take care of myself."

"You don't have to say it like that," he said. "I'm putting myself out for you right now."

Imagine this: a sweet house sits on the outskirts of a town in Alabama. One night, eight-year-old Jule wakes up in the dark. Did she hear a noise?

She isn't sure. The house is quiet.

She goes downstairs in a thin pink nightgown.

On the ground floor, a spike of cold fear goes through her. The living room is trashed, books and papers everywhere. The office is even worse. File cabinets have been tipped over. The computers are gone.

"Mama? Papa?" Little Jule runs back upstairs to look in her parents' room.

Their beds are empty.

Now she is truly frightened. She slams open the bathroom. They aren't there. She sprints outside.

The yard is ringed with looming trees. Little Jule is halfway down the walkway when she realizes what she's seeing there, in the circle of light created by a streetlamp.

Mama and Papa lie in the grass, facedown. Their bodies are crumpled and limp. The blood pools black underneath them. Mama has been shot through the brain. She must have died instantly. Papa is clearly dead, but the only injuries Jule can see are on his arms. He must have bled out from his wounds. He is curled around Mama, as if he thought of only her in his last moments.

Jule runs back into the house to call the police. The phone line is disconnected.

She returns to the yard, wanting to say a prayer, thinking

to say goodbye, at least—but her parents' bodies have disappeared. Their killer has taken them away.

She does not let herself cry. She sits for the rest of the night in that circle of light from the streetlamp, soaking her nightgown in thickening blood.

For the next two weeks, Little Jule is alone in that ransacked house. She stays strong. She cooks for herself and sorts through the papers left behind, looking for clues. As she reads the documents, she pieces together lives of heroism, power, and secret identities.

One afternoon she is in the attic, looking at old photographs, when a woman in black appears in the room.

The woman steps forward, but Little Jule is quick. She throws a letter opener, hard and fast, but the woman catches it left-handed. Little Jule climbs a pile of boxes, grabs an overhead attic beam, and pulls herself onto it. She runs across the beam and squeezes through a high window onto the roof. Panic thuds in her chest.

The woman takes after her. Jule leaps from the roof to the branches of a neighboring tree and breaks off a sharp stick to use as a weapon. She holds it in her mouth as she climbs down. She is sprinting into the underbrush when the woman shoots her in the ankle.

The pain is intense. Little Jule is sure that her parents' killer has come to finish her off—but the woman in black helps her up and tends the wound. She removes the bullet and treats the injury with antiseptic.

As she bandages, the woman explains that she is a recruiter. She has been watching these past two weeks. Not only is Jule the child of two exceptionally skilled people, she is a remarkable intellect with a fierce survival instinct. The woman wants to train Jule and help her seek revenge. Since she is something of a long-lost aunt. She knows the secrets those parents kept from their beloved only daughter.

Here begins a highly unusual education. Jule goes to a specialized academy housed in a renovated mansion on an ordinary street in New York City. She learns surveillance techniques, performs backflips, and masters the removal of handcuffs and straitjackets. She wears leather pants and loads her pockets with gadgets. There are lessons in foreign languages, social customs, literature, martial arts, the use of firearms, disguises, various accents, methods of forgery, and fine points of the law. The education lasts ten years. By the time it is complete, Jule has become the kind of woman it would be a great mistake to underestimate.

That was the origin story of Jule West Williams. By the time she was living at the Playa Grande, Jule preferred it to any other story she might tell about herself.

Donovan stopped and opened the driver's-side door. The light came on inside the car.

"Where are we?" Jule asked. It was dark outside.

"San José del Cabo."

"This where you live?"

"Not too close."

Jule was relieved, but it seemed very black out. Shouldn't there be streetlights and businesses, lit up for the tourist crowd? "Anyone nearby?" she asked.

"I parked in an alley so you wouldn't be seen getting out of my car."

Jule crawled out. Her muscles were stiff and her face felt coated in grease. The alley was lined with garbage bins. There was light only from a couple of second-story windows. "Thanks for the ride. Pop the trunk, will you?"

"You said a hundred dollars American when I got you to town."

"Of course." Jule took her wallet from her back pocket and paid.

"But now it's more," Donovan added.

"What?"

"Three hundred more."

"I thought we were friends."

He took a step toward her. "I make you drinks because it's my job. I pretend to like talking to you, because that's my job, too. You think I don't see how you look down at me? Second-best Hulk. What kind of scotch. We're not friends, Ms. Williams. You're lying to me half the time, and I'm lying to you all the time." She could smell liquor spilled on his shirt. His breath was hot in her face.

Jule had honestly believed he liked her. They had shared jokes and he'd given her free potato chips. "Wow," she said quietly.

"Another three hundred," he said.

Was he a small-time hustler jacking a girl who was carrying a lot of American dollars? Or was he a sleazeball who thought she'd rub up against him rather than give him the extra three hundred? Could Noa have paid him off?

Jule tucked her wallet back in her pocket. She shifted the strap so her bag went across her chest. "Donovan?" She stepped forward, close. She looked up at him with big eyes.

Then she brought her right forearm up hard, snapped his head back, and punched him in the groin. He doubled over. Jule grabbed his slick hair and yanked his head back. She twisted him around, forcing him off balance.

He jabbed with one elbow, slamming Jule in the chest. It hurt, but the second thrust of the elbow missed as she sidestepped, grabbed that elbow, and twisted it behind Donovan's back. His arm was soft, repulsive. She held on tight and with her free hand snatched her money out of his greedy fingers.

She shoved the cash into her jeans pocket and jerked Donovan's elbow hard while she tapped his hip pockets, looking for his phone.

Not there. Back pocket, then.

She found it and shoved the phone down her bra for lack of anywhere else. Now he couldn't call Noa with her location, but he still had the car keys in his left hand.

Donovan kicked out, hitting her in the shin. Jule punched him in the side of the neck and he crumpled forward. One hard shove and Donovan hit the ground. He started to push himself up, but Jule grabbed a metal lid from one of the nearby trash cans and banged it on his head twice and he collapsed on a pile of garbage bags, bleeding from the forehead and one eye.

Jule backed out of his reach. She still held the lid. "Drop your keys."

Moaning, Donovan extended his left hand and tossed them so they landed a couple of inches from his body.

Jule grabbed the keys and popped the trunk. Then she took her rolling suitcase and sprinted down the street before Donovan could stand up.

She slowed to a walk as soon as she hit the main road in San José del Cabo and checked her shirt. It looked clean enough. She wiped her hand slowly and calmly over her face, in case there was anything on it—dirt, spit, or blood. She pulled a compact out of her bag and checked herself as she moved, using the mirror to look over her shoulder.

There was no one behind her.

She put on matte pink lipstick, snapped her compact shut, and slowed her pace even more.

She couldn't look like she was running from anything.

The air was warm, and music thumped from inside the bars. Tourists milled around in front of many of them—white, black, and Mexican, all drunk and loud. Cheap vacation crowds. Jule tossed Donovan's keys and phone in a trash can. She looked for a cab or a supercabos bus but didn't see either.

Okay, then.

She needed to hide and change, in case Donovan came after her. He would pursue her if he was working for Noa. Or if he wanted revenge.

Picture yourself, now, on film. Shadows flit across your smooth skin as you walk. There are bruises forming underneath your clothes, but your hair looks excellent. You're armed with gadgets, thin shards of metal that perform outrageous feats of technology and assault. You carry poisons and antidotes.

You are the center of the story. You and no one else. You've got that interesting origin tale, that unusual education. Now you're ruthless, you're brilliant, you're practically fearless. There's a body count behind you, because you do whatever's required to stay alive—but it's a day's work, that's all.

You look superb in the light from the Mexican bar windows. After a fight, your cheeks are flushed. And oh, your clothes are so very flattering.

Yes, it's true that you are criminally violent. Brutal, even. But that's your job and you're uniquely qualified, so it's sexy.

Jule watched a shit-ton of movies. She knew that women were rarely the centers of such stories. Instead, they were eye candy, arm candy, victims, or love interests. Mostly, they existed to help the great white hetero hero on his fucking epic journey. When there *was* a heroine, she weighed very little, wore very little, and had had her teeth fixed.

Jule knew she didn't look like those women. She would never look like those women. But she was everything those heroes were, and in some ways, she was more.

She knew that, too.

She reached the third Cabo bar and ducked inside. It was furnished with picnic tables and had taxidermied fish on the walls. The customers were mainly Americans, getting sloshed after a day of sport fishing. Jule pushed quickly to the back, glanced over her shoulder, and went into the men's room.

It was empty. She ducked into a stall. Donovan would never look for her here.

The toilet seat was wet and coated yellow. Jule dug in her suitcase until she found a black wig—a sleek bob with bangs. She put it on, wiped off her lipstick, applied a dark gloss, and powdered her nose. She buttoned a black cotton cardigan over her white T-shirt.

A guy came in and used the urinal. Jule stood still, glad she was wearing jeans and heavy black boots. Only her feet and the bottom of her suitcase would be visible at the low edge of the stall.

A second guy came in and used the stall next to hers. She looked at his shoes.

It was Donovan.

Those were his dirty white Crocs. Those were his nurse-like Playa Grande trousers. Jule's blood pounded in her ears.

She quietly picked her suitcase up off the floor and held it so he couldn't see it. She stayed motionless.

Donovan flushed and Jule heard him shuffle to the sink. He ran the water.

Another guy came in. "Could I borrow your phone?" Donovan asked in English. "Just a quick call."

"Someone beat you up, man?" The other guy had an American accent, Californian. "You look like you been through it."

"I'm fine," said Donovan. "I just need a phone."

"I don't have calls here, just texting," the guy said. "I have to get back to my buddies."

"I'm not going to steal it," said Donovan. "I just need to—"

"I said no, okay? But I wish you well, dude." The other guy left without using the facilities.

Did Donovan want the phone because he had no car keys and needed a ride? Or because he wanted to call Noa?

He breathed heavily, as if in pain. He didn't run the water again.

Finally, he left.

Jule set the suitcase down. She shook her hands to get the blood moving again and stretched her arms behind her back. Still in the stall, she counted her money, both pesos and dollars. She checked her wig in her compact mirror.

When she felt certain Donovan was gone, Jule walked out of the men's room, confident, no big thing, and headed for the street. Outside, she pushed through the crowds of partiers to a corner and found herself in luck. A taxi pulled up. She jumped in and asked for the Grand Solmar, the resort next to Playa Grande.

At the Grand Solmar she got a second taxi easily. She asked the new driver to take her to a cheap, locally owned place in town. He drove her to the Cabo Inn.

It was a dive. Cheap walls, dirty paint, plastic furniture, plastic flowers on the counter. Jule checked in under a false name and paid the clerk in pesos. He didn't ask for ID.

Up in the room, she used the small coffeemaker to brew a cup of decaf. She put three sugars in. She sat on the edge of the bed.

Did she need to run?

No.

Yes.

No.

Nobody knew where she was. No one on earth. That fact should have made her happy. She had wanted to disappear, after all.

But she felt afraid.

She wished for Paolo. Wished for Imogen.

Wished she could undo everything that had happened.

If only she could go back in time, Jule felt, she would be a better person. Or a different person. She would be more herself. Or maybe less herself. She didn't know which, because she didn't any longer know what shape her own self was, or whether there was really no Jule at all, but only a series of selves she presented for different contexts.

Were all people like that, with no true self?

Or was it only Jule?

She didn't know if she could love her own mangled, strange heart. She wanted someone else to do it for her, to see it beating behind her ribs and to say, *I can see your true self. It is there, and it is rare and worthy. I love you.*

How dark and stupid it was to be mangled and strange, to be no particular shape, to have no self when life was stretching out before her. Jule had many rare talents. She worked hard and really had so damn much to offer. She knew all that.

So why did she feel worthless at the same time?

She wanted to call Imogen. She wished she could hear Immie's low laugh and her run-on sentences spilling out secrets. She wished she could say to Imogen, *I'm scared.* And Immie would say, *But you're brave, Jule. You're the bravest person I know.*

She wished Paolo would come and put his arms around her, telling her as he had once that she was *a top-notch, excellent person.*

She wanted there to be someone who loved her unconditionally, someone who would forgive her anything. Or better, someone who knew everything already and loved her for it.

Neither Paolo nor Immie was capable of that.

Still, Jule remembered the feel of Paolo's lips on hers, and the smell of Immie's jasmine perfume.

Wearing the black wig, Jule went downstairs to the Cabo Inn's business office. She had thought out her strategy. The office was closed this time of night, but she tipped the desk clerk to open it for her. On the computer, she booked a flight out of San José del Cabo to Los Angeles for the next morning. She used her own name and charged it on her usual credit card, the same one she'd been using at the Playa Grande.

Then she asked the clerk where she could buy a car for cash. He said there was a dealer who worked out of a backyard who could sell her something in the morning for American dollars. He wrote down an address, on Ortiz off Ejido, he said.

Noa was tracking credit cards. She had to be, or she'd never have found Jule. Now the detective would see the new charge and go to LA. Jule herself would buy a car for cash and drive toward Cancùn. From Cancùn, she'd make her way eventually to the island of Culebra in Puerto Rico, where there were loads of Americans who never showed their passports to anyone.

She thanked the clerk for the information about the car dealer. "You're not going to remember our conversation, are you?" she said, pushing another twenty across the counter to him.

"I might," he said.

"No you won't." She added a fifty.

"I never saw you," he said.

The sleep was bad. Even worse than usual. Dreams of drowning in warm turquoise water; dreams of abandoned cats walking across her body as she slept; dreams of strangulation by serpent. Jule woke up screaming.

She drank water. Took a cold shower.

Slept and woke up screaming again.

At five a.m., she stumbled to the bathroom, splashed water on her face, and lined her eyes. Why not? She liked makeup. She had time. She layered concealer and powder, added smoky shadow, then mascara and a nearly black lipstick with a gloss over it.

She rubbed gel into her hair and got dressed. Black jeans, boots again, and a dark T-shirt. Too warm for the Mexican heat, but practical. She packed her suitcase, drank a bottle of water, and stepped out the door.

Noa was sitting in the hallway, her back against the wall, holding a steaming cup of coffee between her hands.

Waiting.

Seven weeks earlier, at the end of April, Jule woke up in a youth hostel on the outskirts of London. There were eight bunks to a room: thin mattresses, topped with regulation white sheets. Sleeping bags lay on top of those. Backpacks leaned against the walls. There was a faint reek of body odor and patchouli.

She'd slept in her workout clothes. She eased out of bed, laced her shoes, and ran eight miles through the suburb, past pubs and butcher shops that were still shuttered in the early light. On return, she did planks, lunges, push-ups, and squats in the hostel common room.

Jule was in the shower before her roommates woke up and started using the hot water. Then she climbed back into her top bunk and unwrapped a chocolate protein bar.

The bunk room was still dark. She opened *Our Mutual Friend* and read by the light on her phone. It was a thick Victorian novel about an orphan. Charles Dickens wrote it. Her friend Imogen had given it to her.

Imogen Sokoloff was the best friend Jule had ever had.

Her favorite books were always about orphans. Immie was an orphan herself, born in Minnesota to a teenage mama who had died when Immie was two. Then she'd been adopted by a couple who lived in a penthouse on New York's Upper East Side.

Patti and Gil Sokoloff were in their late thirties at the time. They couldn't have children, and Gil's legal work had long included volunteer advocacy for kids in the foster care system. He believed in adoption. So, after several years on wait lists for a newborn baby, the Sokoloffs declared themselves open to taking an older child.

They fell in love with this particular two-year-old's fat arms and freckled nose. They took her in, renamed her Imogen, and left her old name in a file cabinet. She was photographed and tickled. Patti cooked her hot macaroni with butter and cheese. When little Immie was five, the Sokoloffs sent her to the Greenbriar School, a private establishment in Manhattan. There, she wore a uniform of green and white and learned to speak French. On weekends, little Immie played Lego, baked cookies, and went to the American Museum of Natural History, where she loved the reptile skeletons best. She celebrated all the Jewish holidays and, when she grew up, had an unorthodox bat mitzvah ceremony in the woods upstate.

The bat mitzvah became complicated. Patti's mother and Gil's parents did not consider Imogen Jewish, because her biological mother had not been. They all pushed for a formal conversion process that would put off the ceremony for a year, but instead Patti left the family synagogue and joined a secular Jewish community that did ceremonies at a mountain retreat.

Thus it was that at age thirteen, Imogen Sokoloff became more conscious of her orphan status than she ever had been before, and began reading the stories that would become a touchstone of her interior life. At first she went back to the orphan books she'd been pushed to read in school. There were a lot of those. "I liked the clothes and puddings and the horse-drawn carriages," Immie told Jule.

Back in June, the two of them had been living together in a house Immie rented on the island of Martha's Vineyard. That day, they drove to a farm stand where you could pick your own flowers. "I liked *Heidi* and God knows what other dreck," Immie told Jule. She was bent over a dahlia bush with a pair of scissors. "But later, all those books made me puke. The heroines were so effing cheerful all the time. They were paragons of self-sacrificing womanhood. Like, 'I'm starving to death! Here, eat my only bakery bun!' 'I can't walk, I'm paralyzed, but still I see the bright side of life, happy happy!' *A Little Princess* and *Pollyanna,* let me tell you, they are selling you a pack of ugly lies. Once I realized that, I was pretty much over them."

Finished with her bouquet, Immie climbed up to sit on the wooden fence. Jule was still picking flowers.

"In high school I read *Jane Eyre, Vanity Fair, Great Expectations,* et cetera," Immie went on. "They're, like, the edgy orphans."

"The books you gave me," Jule said, realizing.

"Yeah. Like, in *Vanity Fair,* Becky Sharp is one big

ambition machine. She'll stop at zero. Jane Eyre has temper tantrums, throws herself on the floor. Pip in *Great Expectations* is deluded and money hungry. All of them want a better life and go after it, and all of them are morally compromised. That makes them interesting."

"I like them already," said Jule.

Immie had gotten into Vassar College on the strength of her essay about those characters. She wasn't much for school besides that, she admitted. She didn't like it when people told her what to do. When professors assigned her to read the ancient Greeks, she had not done it. When her friend Brooke told her to read Suzanne Collins, she had not done that, either. And when her mother told her to work harder on her studies, Immie had dropped out of school.

Of course the pressure hadn't been the only reason Immie left Vassar. The situation was desperately complicated. But Patti Sokoloff's controlling nature was definitely a factor.

"My mother believes in the American dream," said Imogen. "And she wants me to believe in it, too. Her parents were born in Belarus. They full-on bought the package. You know, that idea that here in the US of A, anyone can reach the top. Doesn't matter where you start out, one day, you can run the country, get rich, own a mansion. Right?"

This conversation happened a little later in the Martha's Vineyard summer. Jule and Immie were at Moshup Beach. They had a large cotton blanket spread underneath them.

"It's a pretty dream," said Jule, popping a potato chip into her mouth.

"My dad's family bought it, too," Immie continued. "His grandparents came from Poland and they lived in these tenements. Then his father did well and owned a delicatessen. My dad was supposed to move even further up, be the first in his family to go to college, so he did exactly that. He became, like, this big lawyer. His parents were so proud. It seemed simple to them: Leave the old country behind and reinvent your life. And if *you* couldn't quite live the American dream, then your children would do it for you."

Jule loved hearing Immie talk. She hadn't ever met anyone who spoke so freely. Immie's dialogue was rambling, but it was also relentlessly curious and thoughtful. She didn't seem to censor herself or craft her sentences. She just talked, in a flow that made her seem alternately questioning and desperate to be heard.

"Land of opportunity," Jule said now, just to see what direction Immie would go.

"That's what they believe, but I don't think it's really true," Immie responded. "Like, you can figure out from half an hour of watching the news that there's more opportunity for white people. And for people who speak English."

"And for people with your kind of accent."

"East Coast?" said Immie. "Yeah, I guess. And for non-disabled people. Oh, and men! Men, men, men! Men still walk around like the US of A is a big cake store and all the cake is for them. Don't you think?"

"I'm not letting them have my cake," said Jule. "That's my bloody cake and I'm eating it."

"Yes. You defend your cake," said Immie. "And you get chocolate cake with chocolate icing and, like, five layers. But for me, the point is—go ahead and call me stupid, but I don't want cake. Maybe I'm not even hungry. I'm trying to just *be*. To exist and enjoy what's right in front of me. I know that's a luxury and I'm probably an asshole for even having that luxury, but I also think, I'm trying to appreciate it, people! Let me just be grateful that I'm here on this beach, and not feel like I'm supposed to be *striving* all the time."

"I think you're wrong about the American dream," said Jule.

"No, I'm not. Why?"

"The American dream is to be an action hero."

"Seriously?"

"Americans like to fight wars," said Jule. "We want to change laws or break them. We like vigilantes. We're crazy about them, right? Superheroes and the *Taken* movies and whatever. We're all about heading out west and grabbing land from people who had it before. Slaughtering the so-called bad guys and fighting the system. That's the American dream."

"Tell that to my mom," said Immie. "Say, *Hello! Immie wants to grow up to be a vigilante, rather than a captain of industry.* See how it goes."

"I'll have a talk with her."

"Good. That'll fix everything." Immie chuckled and rolled over on the beach blanket. She took off her sunglasses. "She has ideas about me that don't fit. Like, when I was a kid, it would have been a huge deal to me to have a couple friends who were also adopted, so I didn't feel alone or different or whatever, but back then she was all, *Immie's fine, she doesn't need that, we're just like other families!* Then five hundred years later, in ninth grade, she read a magazine article about adopted kids and decided I had to be friends with this girl Jolie, this girl who'd just started at Greenbriar."

Jule remembered. The girl from the birthday party and American Ballet Theatre.

"My mom had fantasies about the two of us bonding, and I tried, but that girl seriously did *not* like me," Immie continued. "She had blue hair. Very cooler-than-thou. She teased me for my whole thing about stray cats, and for reading *Heidi,* and she made fun of the music I liked. But *my* mom kept calling *her* mom, and her mom kept calling my mom, making plans for the two of us. They imagined this whole adopted-kid connection between us that never existed." Imogen sighed. "It was just sad. But then she moved to Chicago and my mom let it go."

"Now you have me," said Jule.

Immie reached up to touch the back of Jule's neck. "Now I have you, which makes me significantly less mental."

"Less mental is good."

Immie opened the cooler and found two bottles of homemade iced tea. She always packed drinks for the beach. Jule didn't like the lemon slices floating in it, but she drank some anyway.

"You look pretty with your hair cut short," Immie said, touching Jule's neck again.

On her winter break from her first year at Vassar, Imogen had rummaged in Gil Sokoloff's file cabinet, looking for her adoption records. They weren't hard to find. "I guess I thought reading the file would give me some insight into my identity," she said. "Like learning names would explain why I was so miserable in college, or make me feel grounded in some way I never had. But no."

That day, Immie and Jule had driven to Menemsha, a fishing village not far from Immie's Vineyard house. They had walked out onto a stone pier that stretched into the sea. Gulls wheeled overhead. Water lapped at their feet. They were the same height, and as they sat on the rocks, their legs were tan in front of them, shiny with sunblock.

"Yeah, it was total poop," said Imogen. "There was no dad listed at all."

"What was your birth name?"

Immie blushed and pulled her hoodie up over her face for a moment. She had deep dimples and even teeth. Her pixie-cut bleached hair showed her tiny ears, one of which was triple pierced. Her eyebrows were plucked into thin lines.

"I don't want to say," she told Jule from inside the fabric. "I'm hiding in my hoodie now."

"Come on. You started the story."

"You can't laugh if I tell you." Immie lifted the hoodie and looked at Jule. "Forrest laughed and then I got mad. I didn't forgive him for two days until he brought me lemon cream chocolates." Forrest was Immie's boyfriend. He lived with them in the Martha's Vineyard house.

"Forrest could learn manners," said Jule.

"He didn't think. He just blurted out the laugh. Then he was super sorry afterward." Immie always defended Forrest after criticizing him.

"Please tell me your birth name," said Jule. "I will not laugh."

"Promise?"

"I promise."

Immie whispered in Jule's ear, "Melody, and then Bacon. Melody Bacon."

"Was there a middle name?" Jule asked.

"Nope."

Jule did not laugh, or even smile. She put both her arms around Immie's body. They looked out at the sea. "Do you *feel* like a Melody?"

"No." Immie was thoughtful. "But I don't feel like an Imogen, either."

They watched a pair of seagulls that had just landed on a rock near them.

"Why did your mother die?" Jule asked eventually. "Was that in the file?"

"I guessed the basic picture before I read it, but yeah. She overdosed on meth."

Jule took that in. She pictured her friend as a toddler in a wet diaper, crawling across dirty bedclothes while her mother lay beneath them, high and neglectful. Or dead.

"I have two marks on my upper right arm," said Immie. "I had them when I came to live in New York. As far as I knew, I'd always had them. I never thought to ask, but the nurse at Vassar told me they were burns. Like from a cigarette."

Jule didn't know what to say. She wanted to fix things for baby Immie, but Patti and Gil Sokoloff had already done that, long ago.

"My parents are dead, too," she said, finally. It was the first time she'd spoken it aloud, though Immie already knew she'd been raised by her aunt.

"I figured," said Immie. "But I also figured you didn't want to talk about it."

"I don't," said Jule. "Not yet, anyway." She leaned forward, separating herself from Imogen. "I don't know what story to tell about it yet. It doesn't . . ." Words failed her. She couldn't ramble like Immie did, to figure herself out. "The story won't take shape."

It was true. At that time, Jule had only begun to construct the origin tale she would later rely upon, and she could not, could not tell anything else.

"All good," said Imogen.

She reached into her backpack and pulled out a thick bar of milk chocolate. She unwrapped it halfway and broke off a piece for Jule and a piece for herself. Jule leaned back against the rock and let the chocolate melt in her mouth and the sun warm her face. Immie shooed the begging seagulls away, scolding them.

Jule felt then that she knew Imogen completely. Everything was understood between them, and it always would be.

Now, in the youth hostel, Jule put down *Our Mutual Friend*. There was a body in the Thames, early in the story. She didn't like reading that—the description of a waterlogged dead body. Jule's days were long now, since news had gotten around that Imogen Sokoloff had killed herself in that selfsame river, weighting her pockets with stones and jumping off the Westminster Bridge, leaving a suicide note in her bread box.

Jule thought about Immie every day. Every hour. She remembered the way Immie covered her face with her hands or her hoodie when she felt vulnerable. The high, bubble-gum sound of her voice. Imogen rolled her rings around her fingers. She had those two cigarette burns on her upper arm and a scar on one hand from a hot pan of cream-cheese brownies. She chopped onions fast and hard with an outsize heavy knife, something she had learned to do from a cooking video. She smelled like jasmine and sometimes like coffee with cream and sugar. There was a lemony spray she put on her hair.

Imogen Sokoloff was the type of girl teachers never thought worked to her full potential. The type of girl who blew off studying and yet filled her favorite books with sticky notes. Immie refused to strive for greatness or to work toward other people's definitions of success. She struggled to wrest herself from men who wanted to dominate her and women who wanted her exclusive attention. She refused, over and over, to give any single person her devotion, preferring instead to make a home for herself that she defined on her own terms, and of which she was master. She had accepted her parents' money but not their control of her identity, and had taken advantage of her good fortune to reinvent herself, to find a different way of living. It was a particular kind of bravery, one that often got mistaken for selfishness or laziness. She was the type of girl you might think was nothing more than a private-school blonde, but you'd be very wrong if you went no deeper than that.

Today, when the hostel woke up and the backpackers began staggering to the bathroom, Jule went out. She spent the day as she often did, on self-improvement. She walked through the halls of the British Museum for a couple of hours, learning the names of paintings and drinking a series of Diet Cokes from small bottles. She stood in a bookshop for an hour and committed a map of Mexico to memory, then learned by heart a chapter of a book called *Wealth Management: Eight Core Principles.*

She wanted to call Paolo, but she could not.

She wouldn't answer any calls except the one she was waiting for.

The phone rang as Jule came out of the tube near the hostel. It was Patti Sokoloff. Jule saw the cell number and used her general American accent.

Patti was in London, it turned out.

Jule was not expecting that.

Could Jule meet for lunch at the Ivy tomorrow?

Of course. Jule said how surprised she was to hear from Patti. They had spoken a number of times directly after Immie's death, when Jule had talked to police officers and shipped back items from Immie's London flat while Patti nursed Gil in New York City, but all those difficult conversations had finished some weeks ago.

Patti normally had a busy, chatty way about her, but today she sounded low and her voice didn't have its usual animation. "I should tell you," she said, "that I lost Gil."

That was a shock. Jule thought of Gil Sokoloff's swollen gray face and the funny little dogs he doted on. She had liked him very much. She hadn't known he was dead.

Patti explained that Gil had died two weeks ago of heart failure. All those years of kidney dialysis, and his heart had killed him. Or maybe, Patti said, because of Immie's suicide, he had not wanted to continue living any longer.

They talked about Gil's illness for a while, and about how wonderful he was, and about Immie. Patti said what a help Jule had been, handling things in London when the Sokoloffs couldn't leave New York. "I know it seems strange for me to be traveling," Patti said, "but after all those years of looking after Gil, I can't bear to be in the apartment alone. It's filled

41

with his things, Immie's things. I was going to . . ." Her voice trailed off, and when she started talking again it was forced and bright. "Anyway, my friend Rebecca lives in Hampshire and she offered me use of her guest cottage to rest up and heal. She told me I had to come. Some friends are just like that. I hadn't talked to Rebecca in ages, but the moment she called—after hearing about Immie and Gil—we started up again right away. No small talk. It was all honesty. We went to Greenbriar together. School friends have these memories, these shared histories that bind them together, I think. Look at you and Immie. You picked up again so brilliantly after being apart."

"I'm very, very sorry about Gil," Jule said. She meant it completely.

"He was sick forever. So many pills." Patti paused, and when she went on she sounded choked. "I think after what happened to Immie, he just had no fight left in his body. He and Immie, they were my sweetie potatoes." Then she pushed her voice again into busy brightness: "Now, back to the reason I called. You'll come to lunch, right?"

"I said I'd come. Of course."

"The Ivy, tomorrow at one. I want to thank you for all you did for me, and for Gil, after Immie died. And I even have a surprise for you," said Patti. "Something that might actually cheer us both up. So don't be late."

When the conversation was over, Jule held the phone to her chest for a while.

The Ivy inhabited its narrow corner of London perfectly. It seemed custom-fit to its plot of land. Inside, the walls were lined with portraits and stained glass. It smelled like money: roasted lamb and hothouse flowers. Jule wore a fitted dress and ballet flats. She had added red lipstick to her college-girl makeup.

She found Patti waiting for her at a table, drinking water from a wineglass. When Jule had last seen her eleven months ago, Immie's mother had been a glossy woman. She was a dermatologist, midfifties, trim except for a potbelly. Her skin had had a moist pinkish sheen, and her hair had been long, dyed deep brown and ironed into loose curls. Now the hair was gray at the roots and chopped into a bob. Her mouth looked swollen and manly without lipstick. She wore, as women of the Upper East Side do, narrow black pants and a long cashmere cardigan—but instead of heels, she had on a pair of bright blue running shoes. Jule almost didn't recognize her. Patti stood and smiled as Jule came across the room. "I look different, I know."

"No you don't," Jule lied. She kissed Patti's cheek.

"I can't do it any longer," said Patti. "All that time in front of the mirror in the morning, the uncomfortable shoes. Putting on the face."

Jule sat down.

"I used to put on my face for Gil," Patti went on. "And for Immie, when she was little. She used to say, 'Mommy, curl your hair! Go put on sparkles!' Now there's no reason.

I'm taking time off work. One day I thought, *I don't have to bother.* I walked out the door without doing anything and it was such a relief, I can't say. But I do know it disturbs people. My friends worry. But I think, meh. I lost Imogen. I lost Gil. This is me now."

Jule was anxious to say the right thing, but she didn't know if sympathy or distraction was required. "I read a book about that in college," she said.

"About what?"

"The presentation of self in everyday life. This guy Goffman had the idea that in different situations, you perform yourself differently. Your character isn't static. It's an adaptation."

"I have stopped performing myself, you mean?"

"Or you're doing it another way now. There are different versions of the self."

Patti picked up the menu, then reached over and touched Jule's hand. "You need to go back to college, sweetie potato. You're so smart."

"Thank you."

Patti looked Jule in the eye. "I'm very intuitive about people, you know," she said, "and you have so much potential. You're hungry and adventurous. I hope you know you could be anything in the world you want."

The waiter arrived and took a drink order. Someone else set down a bread basket.

"I brought you Imogen's rings," said Jule, when the bustle was over. "I should have mailed them back before, but I—"

"I get it," said Patti. "It was hard to let them go."

Jule nodded. She handed over a package of tissue paper. Patti pulled the sticky tape off. Inside lay eight antique rings, all carved or shaped like animals. Immie had collected them. They were funny and unusual, carefully crafted, all different styles. The ninth one, Jule still wore. Immie had given it to her. It was a jade snake on her right ring finger.

Patti began to weep quietly into her napkin.

Jule looked down at the collection. Each of those circles had been on Immie's fragile fingers at one point or another. Immie had stood, sun-kissed, in that jewelry store on the Vineyard. "I want to see the most unusual ring you have for sale," she'd said to the shopkeeper. And later, "This one is for you." She'd given Jule the snake ring, and Jule would not stop wearing it, now, even though she didn't deserve it any longer, and maybe had never deserved it at all.

Jule gagged, a feeling that came from deep in her stomach and rippled through her throat. "Excuse me." She got up and stumbled toward the ladies' toilet. The restaurant spun around her. Black closed in from the sides of her eyes. She clutched the back of an empty chair to steady herself.

She was going to be sick. Or faint. Or both. Here in the Ivy, surrounded by these pristine people, where she didn't deserve to be, embarrassing the poor, poor mother of a friend she hadn't loved well enough, or had loved too much.

Jule reached the restroom and stood bent over the sink.

The gagging would not stop. Her throat contracted over and over.

She closed herself in a stall, steadying herself against the wall. Her shoulders shook. She heaved, but nothing came up.

She stayed in there until the gagging subsided, shaking and trying to catch her breath.

Back at the sink, she wiped her wet face with a paper towel. She pressed her swollen eyes with fingers dipped in cold water.

The red lipstick was in the pocket of her dress. Jule put it on like armor and went back to see Patti.

When Jule returned to the table, Patti had composed herself and was talking to the waiter. "I'll have the beetroot to start," she told him as Jule sat down. "And then the swordfish, I think. The swordfish is good? Yes, okay."

Jule ordered a hamburger and a green salad.

When the waiter left, Patti apologized. "Sorry. I'm very sorry. Are you all right?"

"Sure."

"I warn you, I may cry again later. Possibly on the street! You never know these days. I'm liable to begin sobbing at any given moment." The rings and their tissue paper were no longer on the table. "Listen, Jule," said Patti. "You once told me that your parents failed you. Do you remember?"

Jule did not remember. She never thought of her parents anymore, at all, unless it was through the lens of the hero's origin she had created for herself. She never, ever thought of her aunt.

Now the origin story flashed into her mind: Her parents in the front yard of a pretty little house at the end of a cul-de-sac, in that tiny Alabama town. They lay facedown in pools of black blood that seeped into the grass, lit by a single streetlight. Her mother shot through the brain. Her father bleeding out through bullet holes in his arms.

She found the story comforting. It was beautiful. The parents had been brave. The girl would grow up highly educated and extremely powerful.

But she knew it was not a story to share with Patti. Instead, she said mildly, "Did I say that?"

"Yes, and when you did, I thought maybe I had failed Imogen, too. Gil and I hardly ever talked about her being adopted when she was little. Not in front of her, or in private. I wanted to think of Immie as *my* baby, you know? Not anyone's but mine and Gil's. And it was hard to speak about, because her birth mother became an addict, and there were no family members who would take the baby. I told myself I was protecting her from pain. I had no idea how badly I was failing her until she—" Patti's voice trailed off.

"Imogen loved you," said Jule.

"She was desperate about something. And she didn't come to me."

"She didn't come to me, either."

"I should have raised her so that she could open up to people, get help if she was in trouble."

"Immie told me *everything*," said Jule. "Her secrets, her insecurities, how she wanted to live her life. She told me her birth name. We wore each other's clothes and read each other's books. Honestly, I was very close to Immie when she died, and I think she was mad lucky to have you."

Patti's eyes welled and she touched Jule's hand. "She was lucky to have you, too. I thought so when she first took up with you at Greenbriar freshman year. I know she adored you more than anyone in her life, Jule, because— Well. This is what I wanted to meet with you about. Our family lawyer tells me Immie left you her money."

Jule felt dizzy. She put down her fork.

Immie's money. Millions.

It was safety and power. It was plane tickets and keys to cars, but more importantly, it was tuition payments, food in the larder, medical care. It meant that no one could say no. No one could stop her anymore, and no one could hurt her. Jule wouldn't need help from anyone, ever again.

"I don't understand finance," Patti went on. "I should, I know. But I trusted Gil and I was glad he took care of all that. It bores me out of my skin. But Immie understood it, and she left a will. She sent it to the lawyer before she died. She had a lot of money from her father and me, once she turned eighteen. It was in trust till then, and after her birthday, Gil did the paperwork to shift it over to her."

"She got the money when she was still in high school?"

"The May before college started. Maybe that was a mistake. Anyway, it's done." Patti went on, "She was good with finances. She lived off the interest and never touched the capital except to buy the London flat. That's why she didn't have to work. And in her will, she left it all to you. She made small bequests to the National Kidney Foundation—because of Gil's illness—and to the North Shore Animal League, but she made a will and left *you* the bulk of the money. She sent the lawyer an email that specifically says she wanted to help you go back to college."

Jule was touched. It didn't make sense, but she was.

Patti smiled. "She left this world sending you back to school. That's the bright side I'm trying to see."

"When did she write the will?"

"A few months before she died. She had it notarized in San Francisco. There are just a few things to sign." Patti shoved an envelope across the table. "They'll transfer the money directly into your account, and in September you'll be a sophomore at Stanford."

When the money arrived in her bank, Jule withdrew it all and opened a new checking account somewhere else. She started several new credit card accounts and arranged for the bills to be paid automatically every month.

Then she went shopping. She bought false eyelashes, foundation, liner, blush, powder, brushes, three different lipsticks, two shadows, and a small but expensive makeup box. A red wig, a black dress, and a pair of high heels. More would have been nice, but she needed to travel light.

She used her computer to purchase a plane ticket to Los Angeles, booked an LA hotel, and researched used car dealers in the Las Vegas area. London to LA, then LA by bus to Vegas. From Vegas by car to Mexico. That was the plan.

Jule paged through documents on her laptop. She made sure she knew all the bank numbers, customer service numbers, passwords, credit card numbers, and codes. She memorized passport and driver's license numbers. Then one night, long after dark, she tossed the laptop and her phone into the Thames.

Back at the youth hostel, she wrote a sincere letter of thanks to Patti Sokoloff on an old-fashioned piece of airmail paper and posted it. She cleaned out her storage locker and packed her suitcase. Her identification and papers were neatly organized. She made sure to place all her lotions and hair products in travel-size bottles in sealable plastic bags.

Jule had never been to Vegas. She changed her clothes in the bathroom at the bus station. The sink area was inhabited by a white woman in her fifties with a granny cart. She was sitting on the counter, eating a sandwich wrapped in greasy white paper. She wore dirty black leggings on narrow thighs. Her hair was teased up high, gray and blond. It was matted. Her shoes were on the floor—pale pink vinyl stilettos. Her bare feet, with Band-Aids on the heels, swung in the air.

Jule went into the biggest stall and dug through her case. She put on her hoop earrings for the first time in nearly a year. She wiggled into the dress she'd bought—short and black, paired with leather platform heels. She got out the red wig. It was unnaturally sleek, but the color looked good with her freckles. Jule took out the makeup box, closed her bag, and went to the sink.

The woman sitting on the counter didn't remark on the change of hair color. She crumpled her sandwich wrapper and lit a cigarette.

Jule's makeup skills came from watching online tutorials. For most of the last year she'd been wearing what she thought of as college-girl makeup: natural skin, blush, sheer lips, mascara. Now she brought out fake eyelashes, green shadow, black liner, base, contouring brushes, eyebrow pencil, coral gloss.

It wasn't really necessary. She didn't need the cosmetics, the dress, or the shoes. The wig was probably enough. Still, the transformation was good practice—that was how she thought of it. And she liked becoming someone else.

The other woman spoke as Jule finished her eyes. "You a working girl?"

Jule answered, just for fun, in her Scottish accent. "No."

"I mean, you selling yourself?"

"No."

"Don't sell yourself. So sad, you girls."

"I'm not."

"It's a shame, that's all I'm saying."

Jule was silent. She applied highlighter to her cheekbones.

"I did that job," the woman went on. She lowered herself off the counter and stuffed her messed-up feet into the shoes. "No family anymore and no money: that was how I started, and it's no different now. But it's not a way up, even with high-rolling guys. You should know that."

Jule shrugged into a green cardigan and picked up her case. "Don't worry about me. I'm fine, honestly." Dragging the bag behind her, she headed for the door—but she stumbled slightly in the unfamiliar shoes.

"You all right?" the woman asked.

"Oh, yeah."

"It's hard to be a woman sometimes."

"Yeah, it pretty much sucks, except for the makeup," Jule said. She pushed through the door without looking back.

With her suitcase stashed in a bus-station locker, Jule shouldered a tote bag and took a taxi to the Las Vegas strip. She was tired—she hadn't been able to sleep on the bus ride, and she was on London time.

The casino was lit up with neon, chandeliers, and the sparkle of the slot machines. Jule walked past men in sports jerseys, pensioners, party girls, and a large group of librarians wearing conference badges. It took two hours, walking from place to place, but eventually she found what she was looking for.

There was a cluster of women around a bank of Batman slots having what seemed to be a ridiculously good time. They had frozen drinks, purple and slushy. A couple looked Asian American, a couple white. It was a bachelorette party, and the bride was perfect, just what Jule needed. She was pale and petite, with strong-looking shoulders and gentle freckles—couldn't have been more than twenty-three. Her light brown hair was up in a ponytail, and she wore a hot-pink minidress and a white sash with rhinestones on it: BRIDE TO BE. Dangling from her left shoulder was a small turquoise bag with multiple zippers. She leaned over as her friends played the machines, cheering, comfortable being adored by everyone around her.

Jule walked over to the group and used a lowland Southern accent, like in Alabama. "'Scuse me, do any of y'all— well, my phone's out of charge and I gotta text my friend. I last saw her over by the sushi bar, but then I started playing, and now, whoop! It's three hours later and she's MIA."

The bachelorettes turned around.

Jule smiled. "Oh, are y'all a bridal party?"

"She's getting married on Saturday!" cried one of the women, clutching the bride.

"Hooray!" said Jule. "What's your name?"

"Shanna," said the bride. They were the same height, but Shanna wore flats, so Jule stood over her a little.

"Shanna Dixie, soon to be Shanna McFetridge!" cried a bachelorette.

"Dang," said Jule. "Do you have a dress?"

"Of course I do," said Shanna.

"It's not a Vegas wedding," said a bachelorette. "It's a church wedding."

"Where are y'all from?" asked Jule.

"Tacoma. It's in Washington. You know it? We're just in Vegas for—"

"They planned the whole weekend for me," said Shanna. "We flew in this morning and went to the spa and the nail salon. See? I got the gel. Then we hit the casino, and tomorrow we're gonna see the white tigers."

"And what's your dress? For the wedding, I mean."

Shanna clutched Jule's arm. "It's to die for. I feel like a princess, it's so good."

"Can I see it? On your phone? You must have a picture." Jule put her hand over her mouth and ducked her head a little. "I have a thing about wedding dresses, you know? Ever since I was a bitty girl."

"Hell yes, I have a picture," said Shanna. She unzipped her bag and pulled out a phone in a gold case. The lining of the bag was pink. Inside were a wallet of dark brown leather, two tampons wrapped in plastic, a pack of gum, and a lipstick.

"Lemme see," said Jule. She stepped around to look at Shanna's phone.

Shanna swiped through the pictures. A dog. The rusty underside of a sink. A baby. The same baby again. "That's my boy, Declan. He's eighteen months." Some trees by a lake. "There it is."

The dress was strapless and long, with folds of fabric around the hips. In the picture, Shanna modeled it in a bridal store filled with other white gowns.

Jule oohed and aahed. "Can I see your fiancé?"

"Hell yes. He, like, killed the proposal," said Shanna. "He put the ring in a doughnut. He's in law school. I won't have to work unless I want to." She went on. Talking, talking. She held up the phone to show the lucky guy grinning on the slopes.

"Crazy cute," said Jule. Her hand went into Shanna's bag. She lifted the wallet and slid it into her tote. "My boyfriend, Paolo, is backpacking around the world," she continued. "He's in the Philippines right now. Can you believe it? So I'm in Vegas with my girlfriend. I should get a guy who wants to settle down, not backpack the world, right? If I want a wedding."

"If that's what you want," said Shanna, "you can definitely have it. You can have anything if you set your mind to it. You pray and you, like, visualize."

"Visualization," said one of the bridesmaids. "We went to this workshop. It really works."

"Listen," Jule said. "The reason I came up to talk to y'all

was, could I use your phone? Mine's dead. Would that be okay?"

Shanna handed over her phone and Jule texted a random number. "Meet at 10:15 at the Cheesecake Factory." She handed the phone back to Shanna. "Thanks. You're gonna be the most beautiful bride."

"Same to you, sweetie," said Shanna. "Someday soon."

The bachelorettes waved. Jule waved back and booked it through the lines of slot machines to a bank of elevators.

As soon as the elevator door closed and she was alone, Jule pulled off the wig. She kicked off the heels and pulled joggers and Vans from the tote, yanked the pants on over the short black dress, and slipped the Vans on her feet. The wig and the heels went into the bag. She put on a zip-up hoodie and the doors opened on the tenth floor of the hotel.

Jule didn't get off. As the elevator went back down, she pulled out a makeup wipe and peeled off her false eyelashes. She wiped off her lip gloss. Then she opened Shanna's wallet, snagged the driver's license, and dropped the wallet itself on the floor.

She was another person by the time the doors opened.

Four casinos down on the strip, Jule surveyed six restaurants until she found a place to order a coffee and chat up a lonely college student who was just starting work on the night shift. The place was a 1950s diner replica. The waitress was a tiny woman with freckles and soft brown curls. She wore a polka-dot dress and a frilly housewife's apron. When a crowd of drunk guys barged in talking about beer and burgers, Jule put some cash on the counter to pay for her food and then slid into the kitchen. She snagged the most feminine backpack off a line of hooks and left through a back exit into the casino's service hallway. Running down a flight of stairs and then out into the alley, she shouldered the pack and pushed her way through a group of people lined up for a magic show.

A ways down she rummaged through the bag. In the zipper pocket was a passport. The name on it was Adelaide Belle Perry, age twenty-one.

It was a lucky take. Jule had figured she might have to work a long time before she got a passport. She felt sorry for Adelaide, though, and after taking the passport, she turned the backpack in to a lost properties office.

Back on the strip, she found a wig store and two clothing shops. She stocked up, and by morning, she had moved casinos twice more. Wearing a wavy blond wig and orange lipstick, she lifted the license of one Dakota Pleasance, five foot two. In a black wig and a silver jacket she snagged the passport of Dorothea von Schnell of Germany, five foot three.

By eight a.m., Jule was back in the joggers and Vans, her face wiped clean. She got a cab to the Rio hotel and took the elevator to the roof. She had read about the VooDoo Lounge, fifty-one stories up.

When a battle is over, when he has lived to fight again another day, the great white hetero action hero goes somewhere high above the city, somewhere with a view. Iron Man, Spider-Man, Batman, Wolverine, Jason Bourne, James Bond—they all do it. The hero gazes out at the pain and beauty contained in the twinkling lights of the metropolis. He thinks about his special mission, his unique talents, his strength, his strange, violent life and all the sacrifices he makes to live it.

The VooDoo Lounge early in the morning was little more than a concrete expanse of roof dotted with red and black couches. The chairs were shaped like enormous hands. A staircase curved above the roof. Patrons could climb it for a better view of the Vegas strip below. There were a couple of cages for showgirls to dance in, but no one was in the lounge now except a janitor. He raised his eyebrows as Jule came in. "I just want to have a look," Jule told him. "I'm harmless, I swear."

"Of course you are," he said. "Go ahead. I'm mopping up."

Jule went to the top of the staircase and gazed at the city. She thought of all the lives being led down there. People were buying toothpaste, having arguments, picking up eggs on the way home from work. They lived their lives surrounded by all that glitter and neon, happily assuming that small, cute women were harmless.

Three years ago, Julietta West Williams was fifteen. She'd been in an arcade—a big one, air-conditioned and shiny-new. She was racking up points on a war simulation. She was lost in it, shooting, when two boys she knew from school came up behind her and squeezed her boobs. One on each side.

Julietta elbowed one sharply in his soft stomach, then swung around and stomped hard on the other one's foot. Then she kneed him in the groin.

It was the first time she'd ever hit anyone outside of her martial arts classes. The first time she'd needed to.

All right, she hadn't needed to. She'd wanted to. She enjoyed it.

When that boy bent over, coughing, Jule turned and hit the first one in the face with the heel of her hand. His head flew back and she yanked the front of his T-shirt and yelled into his greasy ear, "I'm not yours to touch!"

She wanted to see fear on that boy's face, and to see his friend crumpled over on a nearby bench. Those two boys had always been so cocky at school, afraid of nothing.

A pimple-face man who worked at the arcade came over and grabbed Julietta's arm. "We can't have fighting in here, miss. I'm afraid you'll have to leave."

"Are you grabbing my arm?" she asked him. "'Cause I don't want you to grab my arm."

He dropped it fast.

He was afraid of her.

He was six inches taller than her and at least three years older. He was a grown man, and he was afraid of her.

It felt good.

Julietta left the arcade. She didn't worry that the boys would follow her. She felt like she was in a movie. She hadn't known she could take care of herself that way, hadn't known that the strength she'd been building in the classes and in the weight room at the high school would pay off. She realized she had built armor for herself. Perhaps that was what she'd been intending to do.

She looked the same, looked just like anyone, but she saw the world differently after that. To be a physically powerful woman—it was something. You could go anywhere, do anything, if you were difficult to hurt.

A few floors down in the Rio hotel hallway, Jule found a maid who was pushing a cart. A forty-dollar tip and she had a room to sleep in until three-thirty. The check-in time was four p.m.

Another night of lifting wallets and another day of sleep and Jule was ready to buy an inconspicuous used car off a sleazy guy in a parking lot. She paid cash. She collected her luggage from the bus station and stashed her extra IDs deep under the felt that lined the hatchback.

She drove herself across the border to Mexico with Adelaide Belle Perry's passport.

16

Three months before Jule arrived in Mexico, Forrest Smith-Martin was on Jule's couch, eating baby carrots with his straight, glossy teeth. He had been staying at her London flat for five nights.

Forrest was Immie's ex-boyfriend. He always acted like he didn't believe a word Jule said. If she said she liked blueberries, he raised his eyebrows like he highly doubted it. If she said Immie had flitted off to Paris, he questioned her about where, precisely, Immie was staying. He made Jule feel illegitimate.

Pale and slim, Forrest belonged to the category of scrawny men who are uncomfortable when women are more muscular than they are. His joints seemed loosely attached, and the woven bracelet around his left wrist looked dirty. He had gone to Yale for world literature. He liked people to know he'd gone to Yale and often brought it up in conversation. He wore little spectacles, was developing a beard that never quite sprouted, and kept his long hair in a man bun on the top of his head. He was twenty-two and working on his novel.

Right now, he was reading a book translated from the French. Albert Camus. He pronounced it *Camoo*. He was draped on the couch, not just sitting, and wore a sweatshirt and his boxer shorts.

Forrest was in the flat because of Immie's death. He said he wanted to sleep on the fold-out couch in the den, to be near Imogen's things. More than once, Jule found him taking Immie's clothes out of the closet and smelling them. A couple of times he hung them from the window frames. He found Imogen's old books—early editions of *Vanity Fair* and other Victorian novels—and piled them next to his bed, as if he needed to see them before he fell asleep. Then he left the toilet seat up.

He and Jule had been handling Immie's death from the London end. Gil and Patti were stuck in New York because of Gil's health. The Sokoloffs had managed to keep the suicide out of all the papers. They said they didn't want publicity, and there was no question of foul play, according to the police. Even though her body hadn't been found, no one doubted what had happened. Immie had left that note in the bread box.

Everyone agreed she must have been depressed. People jumped into the Thames all the time, said the police. If a person weighted herself down before jumping, as Imogen had written she planned to do, there was no telling how long it might take before a body was found.

Now Jule sat next to Forrest and flipped on the TV. It was late-night BBC programming. The two of them had spent the day going through Immie's kitchen, packing things as Patti had requested. It had been a long and emotional project.

"That girl looks like Immie," Forrest said, pointing to an actress on the screen.

Jule shook her head. "I don't think so."

"Yes, she does," said Forrest. "To me, she does."

"Not up close," Jule said. "She just has short hair. People think I look like Immie, too, from a distance."

He looked at her steadily. "You don't look like her, Jule," he said. "Imogen was a million times prettier than you will ever be."

Jule glared. "I didn't know we were getting hostile tonight. I'm kinda tired. Can we just skip it, or are you really jonesing for an argument?"

Forrest leaned toward her, shutting his Camus. "Did Imogen lend you money?" he asked.

"No, she didn't," Jule answered truthfully.

"Did you want to sleep with her?"

"No."

"*Did* you sleep with her?"

"No."

"Did she have a new boyfriend?"

"No."

"There's something you're not telling me."

"There are six hundred things I'm not telling you," Jule said. "Because I'm a private person. And my friend just died. I'm sad and I'm trying to deal with it. Is that all right with you?"

"No," said Forrest. "I need to understand what happened."

"Look. The rule of you staying in this flat is, don't ask Jule a million questions about Immie's private life. Or about Jule's private life. Then we can get along. All right?"

Forrest sputtered. "The rule of this flat? What are you talking about, the rule of this flat?"

"Every place has rules. What you do when you come into a new place is, you figure them out. Like when you're a guest, you learn the codes of behavior and adapt. Yes?"

"Maybe that's what *you* do."

"That's what *everyone* does. You work out how loud you can talk, how you can sit, what things are okay to say and what's rude. It's called being a human in society."

"Nah." Forrest crossed his legs in a leisurely fashion. "I'm not that fake. I just do what feels right to me. And you know what? It's never been a problem, until now."

"Because you're you."

"What does *that* mean?"

"You're a guy. You come from money, you're white, you have really good teeth, you graduated from Yale, the list goes on."

"So?"

"Other people adapt to *you,* asshole. You think there's no adapting going on, but you're fucking blind, Forrest. It's all around you, all the time."

"That's a point," he said. "Okay, I'll grant you that."

"Thank you."

"But if you're thinking through all that lunacy every time you walk into a new situation, then there is something seriously wrong with you, Jule."

"My friend is dead," she told him. "That's what's wrong with me."

Immie hadn't told her secrets to Forrest. She had told them to Jule.

Jule had realized the truth of it early on, even before Immie had told Jule her birth name, and before Brooke Lannon ever turned up at the Vineyard house.

It was the Fourth of July, not long after Jule had first moved in. Immie had found a recipe for pizza dough you made on an outdoor grill. She was messing around with yeast in the kitchen. She had invited friends, summer people she'd met a couple of days earlier at a farmer's market. They came over and ate. Everything was fine, but they wanted to leave early. "Let's drive into town for the fireworks," they said. "We shouldn't miss them. Hurry up."

Jule knew Imogen hated the crush of people at crowded events. She couldn't see over people's heads. There was always too much noise.

Forrest didn't seem to care. He just got in the car with the summer people, stopping only to snag a box of cookies from the pantry.

Jule stayed behind. She and Immie left the dishes for the cleaner and changed into swimsuits. Jule pulled the lid off the hot tub, and Immie brought out tall glasses of seltzer with lemon.

They sat in silence for a bit. The evening had turned cool, and steam rose off the water.

"Do you like it here?" Immie asked finally. "In my house? With me?"

Jule did, and she said so. When Immie looked at her

expectantly, she added: "Every day there's time to actually see the sky, and to taste what I'm eating. There's room to stretch out. No work, no expectations, no adults."

"We're the adults," said Immie, tilting her head back. "I think so, at least. You and me and Forrest, we're the effing adults, and that's why it feels so good. Oops!" She had tipped her seltzer into the hot tub by accident. Now she chased around three slowly sinking pieces of sliced lemon until she caught them. "It's good you like it here," Immie said as she fished the last slice out, "because there was a part of living with Forrest that was like—being alone. I can't explain it. Maybe it's because he's writing a novel, or because he's older than I am. But it's better with you here."

"How did you meet him?"

"In London I went to a summer program with his cousin, and then one day I was getting coffee at Black Dog and I recognized him from Instagram. We started talking. He was here for a month to work on his book. He didn't know anybody. That was that, basically." Immie trailed her fingers across the top of the water. "How about you? You seeing anybody?"

"There were some boyfriends at Stanford," said Jule. "But they're still in California."

"*Some* boyfriends?"

"Three boyfriends."

"Three boyfriends is a lot, Jule!"

Jule shrugged. "I couldn't decide."

"When I first got to college," Immie said, "Vivian Abromowitz invited me to the Students of Color Union party. You've heard me talk about Vivian, right? Anyway, her mom is Chinese American; her dad's Korean Jewish. She was set on going to this party because some guy she crushed on would be there. I was a little nervous about being the only white person, but that turned out fine. The awkward part was that everyone was all political and ambitious. Like, talking about protest rallies and philosophy reading lists and this Harlem Renaissance film series. At a party! I was like, when are we dancing? And the answer was never. Were parties like that at Stanford? With no beer and people being all intellectual?"

"Stanford has a Greek system."

"Okay then, maybe not. Anyway, this tall black guy with dreads, really cute, was like, 'You went to Greenbriar and you haven't read James Baldwin? What about Toni Morrison? You should read Ta-Nehisi Coates.' And I said, 'Hello? I just got to college. I haven't read anybody yet!' Vivian was next to me and she was all, 'Brooke texted me and there's another party that has a DJ, and the rugby team is there. Should we jet?' And I wanted to go to a party where there was dancing. So we left." Immie ducked her head under the water of the hot tub and came back up again.

"What happened with the condescending guy?"

Immie laughed. "Isaac Tupperman. He's why I'm telling this story. I went out with him for nearly two months. That's how come I can remember the names of his favorite writers."

"He was your boyfriend?"

"Yeah. He'd write me poems and leave them on my bicycle. He'd come over late at night, like at two in the morning, and say he missed me. But the pressure was on, too. He grew up in the Bronx and went to Stuy, and he was—"

"What's Stuy?"

"Public school for smart kids in New York. He had a lot of ideas about what I should be, what I should study, what I should care about. He wanted to be the amazing older guy who would enlighten me. And I was flattered, and kind of in awe, but then also sometimes really bored."

"So he was like Forrest."

"What? No. I was so happy when I met Forrest because he was the opposite of Isaac." Immie said it decisively, as if it were completely true. "Isaac liked me because I was ignorant and that meant he could teach me, right? That made him feel like a man. And he did know about a lot of things that I never studied or experienced or whatever. But then—and this is the irony—he was totally annoyed by my ignorance. And in the end, after he broke up with me and I was sad and mental, I came to the Vineyard and one day I thought: *Eff you, Mr. Isaac. I'm not so very ignorant. I just know stuff about stuff that you dismiss as unimportant and useless.* Does that make sense? I mean, I didn't know *Isaac's stuff.* And I do know Isaac's stuff is important, but all the time I spent with him I felt like I was just so dumb and blank. The fact that I couldn't understand his life experience very well, combined with how he was a year ahead of me and really into all his academics, the literary magazine, et cetera—that meant that all the time, he got to be the big man and I was looking up at him with wide eyes. And that was what he liked about me. *And* why he despised me.

"Then there was this week I thought I was pregnant," Immie went on. "Jule, imagine. I'm an adopted kid. And there I am, pregnant with a kid I think I might have to put up for adoption. Or have aborted. The dad is a guy my parents met once and wrote him off as a party person—because of his color and his hairstyle the one time they met him—and I have no idea what to do, so I spend all week skipping class and reading people's abortion stories on the Internet. Then one day I finally get my period and I text Isaac. He drops everything and comes over to my dorm room—and he breaks up with me." Immie put her hands over her face. "I have never been as scared as I was that week," she went on. "When I thought I had a baby inside me."

That night, when Forrest came back from the fireworks, Imogen had already gone to bed. Jule was still awake, watching TV on the living room couch. She followed him as he rummaged in the fridge and found himself a beer and a leftover grilled pork chop. "Do you know how to cook?" she asked him.

"I can boil noodles. And heat up tomato sauce."

"Imogen's really good."

"Yeah. Nice for us, right?"

"She works hard in the kitchen. She taught herself by watching videos and getting cookbooks from the library."

"Did she?" said Forrest, mildly. "Hey, is there crumble left over? Crumble is necessary to my existence right now."

"I ate it," Jule told him.

"Lucky girl," he said. "All right, then. I'm gonna go work on my book. Night is when my brain works best."

One night, after Forrest had been staying with Jule in London for a week, he bought the two of them tickets to see *A Winter's Tale* at the Royal Shakespeare Company. It was something to do. They needed to leave the flat.

They took the Jubilee line to the Central line to St. Paul's and walked toward the theater. It was raining. Since the show didn't start for an hour, they found a pub and ordered fish and chips. The room was dark and the walls were lined with mirrors. They ate at the bar.

Forrest talked a great deal about books. Jule asked him about the Camus he had been reading, *L'Etranger*. She made him explain the plot, which was about a guy with a dead mother who kills another guy and then goes to prison for it.

"It's a mystery?"

"Not at all," said Forrest. "Mysteries perpetuate the status quo. Everything always wraps up at the end. Order is restored. But order doesn't really exist, right? It's an artificial construct. The whole genre of the mystery novel reinforces the hegemony of Western notions of causation. In *L'Etranger*, you know everything that happens from the beginning. There's nothing to find out, because human existence is ultimately meaningless."

"Oh, it's so hot when you say French words," Jule told him, reaching over to his plate and taking a chip. "Not."

When the bill came, Forrest took out his credit card. "My treat, thanks to Gabe Martin."

"Your dad?"

"Yeah. He pays the bills on this baby"—Forrest tapped the card—"till I'm twenty-five. So I can work on my novel."

"Lucky." Jule picked up the card. She memorized the number; she flipped it over and memorized the code on the back. "You don't even see the bill?"

Forrest laughed and took it back. Pushed it across the bar. "Nah. It goes to Connecticut. But I try to stay conscious of my privilege and not take it for granted."

As they walked the rest of the way to the Barbican Centre in the drizzle, Forrest held the umbrella over them both. He bought a program, the kind you can buy in London theaters that's full of photographs and gives a history of the production. They sat down in the dark.

During the intermission, Jule leaned against one wall of the lobby and watched the crowd. Forrest went to the men's room. Jule listened to the accents of the theatergoers: London, Yorkshire, Liverpool. Boston, General American, California. South Africa. London again.

Damn.

Paolo Vallarta-Bellstone was here.

Right now. Across the lobby from Jule.

He seemed very bright in the middle of the drab crowd. He had on a red T-shirt under a sport coat and wore blue-and-yellow track shoes. The bottom edges of his jeans were frayed. Paolo had a Filipina mom and a white hodgepodge American dad. That was how he described them. He had black hair—cut short since she'd seen him last—and gentle-looking eyebrows. Round cheeks, brown eyes, and soft red lips, almost puffy. Straight teeth. Paolo was the type of guy who travels around the world with nothing more than a backpack, who talks to strangers on carousels and in wax museums. He was a conversationalist without pretension. He liked people and always thought the best of them. Right now he was eating Swedish Fish from a small yellow bag.

Jule turned away. She didn't like how happy she felt. She didn't like how beautiful he was.

No. She didn't want to see Paolo Vallarta-Bellstone.

She couldn't see him. Not now, not ever.

She left the lobby promptly and headed back into the theater. The double doors shut behind her. There weren't many audience members in there. Just ushers and a couple of elderly folk who hadn't wanted to leave their seats.

She had to get out as quickly as possible, without seeing Paolo. She grabbed her coat. She wouldn't wait for Forrest.

Was there a side exit somewhere?

She was running up the aisle with her jacket over her arm—and there he was. Standing in front of her. She stopped. There was no getting away from him now.

Paolo waved his bag of Swedish Fish. "Imogen!" He ran the last length of the aisle and kissed her cheek. Jule caught the whiff of sugar on his breath. "I am crazy glad to see you."

"Hello," she said coldly. "I thought you were in Thailand."

"Plans got delayed," Paolo said. "We pushed everything back." He stepped back as if to admire her. "You've got to be the prettiest girl in London. Yowza."

"Thanks."

"I mean it. Woman, not girl. Sorry. Are people following you around, like with their tongues hanging out? How did you get prettier since I last saw you? It's terrifying. I'm talking too much because I'm nervous."

Jule felt her skin warm.

"Come with me," he said. "I'll buy you tea. Or a coffee. Whatever you want. I miss you."

"I miss you, too." She didn't mean to say it. The words came out and they were true.

Paolo grabbed her hand, touching only her fingers. He had always been confident like that. Even though she'd rejected him, he could tell right away that she hadn't meant it. He was supremely gentle and yet sure of himself at the same time. He touched her like the two of them were lucky to be touching each other; like he knew she didn't very often let anyone touch her. Fingertip to fingertip, he led Jule back to the lobby.

"I only didn't call because you told me not to call," Paolo said, letting go of her hand as they stepped into line for tea. "I want to call you all the time. Every day. I stare at my phone and then I don't call because I don't want to be creepy. I'm so glad I ran into you. God, you're pretty."

Jule liked how his T-shirt lay against his collarbone, and the way his wrists moved against the fabric of his jacket. He bit his lower lip when he was worried. His face curved softly against the black of his eyelashes. She wanted to see him first thing in the morning. She felt like if she could just see Paolo Vallarta-Bellstone first thing in the morning, everything would be okay.

"You still don't want to go home to New York?" he asked.

"I don't want to go home, ever," said Jule. Like so many things she found herself saying to him, it was absolutely true. Her eyes filled.

"I don't want to go home, either," he said. Paolo's father was a real estate mogul who had been indicted for insider trading some months ago. It had been all over the news. "My mom left my dad when she found out what he'd been doing. Now she's living with her sister and commuting to work from New Jersey. Things are all mangled with the money

and there are divorce lawyers and criminal lawyers and me-
diators. Ugh."

"I'm sorry."

"It's just ugly. My dad's brother is being a giant racist
about the divorce. You wouldn't believe what's come out of
his mouth. And so my mother is full of venom, frankly. She
has a right to be, but it's hellish to even talk to her on the
phone. I don't think there's anything, really, to go back to."

"What will you do?"

"Travel around some more. My friend will be ready to go
in another couple weeks, and then we'll backpack through
Thailand, Cambodia, and Vietnam, same plan as before.
Then to Hong Kong, and we'll go see my grandmother in
the Philippines." He took Jule's hand again. He ran his finger softly across her palm. "You're not wearing your rings."
Her nails were painted with pale pink polish.

"Just the one." Jule showed him her other hand, which
had the jade viper on it. "The others all belonged to this
friend of mine. I was only borrowing them."

"I thought they were yours."

"No. Yes. No." Jule sighed.

"Which is it?"

"My friend killed herself not that long ago. We argued
and she died angry at me." Jule was telling the truth, and
she was lying. Being with Paolo muddled her thinking. She
knew she shouldn't talk to him anymore. She could feel the
stories she told herself and the stories she told others shift-
ing around, overlapping, changing shades. She couldn't tell,
tonight, what the names of the stories were, what she meant
and what she didn't.

Paolo squeezed her hand. "I'm sorry."

Jule blurted: "Tell me, do you think a person is as bad as her worst actions?"

"What?"

"Do you think a person is as bad as her worst actions?"

"You mean, will your friend go to hell because she killed herself?"

"No." That wasn't what Jule meant at all. "I mean, do our worst actions define us when we're alive? Or do you think human beings are better than the very worst things we have ever done?"

Paolo thought. "Well, take Leontes in *The Winter's Tale*. He tried to poison his friend, he threw his own wife in prison, and he abandoned his baby in the wilderness. So he's the absolute worst. Right?"

"Right."

"But in the end—have you seen it before tonight?"

"No."

"At the end, he's sorry. He's just really, really sorry about everything, and that's enough. Everyone forgives him. Shakespeare lets Leontes be redeemed even though he did all that evil stuff."

Jule wanted to tell Paolo everything.

She wanted to reveal her past to him in its ugliness and beauty, its courage and complexity. She would be redeemed.

She could not speak.

"Ohhh," said Paolo, drawing out the word. "We're not talking about the play, are we?"

Jule shook her head.

"I'm not angry with you, Imogen," said Paolo. "I am crazy about you." He reached out and touched her cheek. Then he ran the pad of his thumb across her lower lip. "I'm sure your friend isn't still angry with you, either, whatever happened when she was alive. You're a top-notch, excellent person. I can tell."

They had reached the front of the line. "Two cups of tea," Jule said to the lady at the counter. Her eyes leaked even though she was not crying. She had to stop being emotional.

"This seems like a dinner conversation," said Paolo. He paid for the tea. "Do you want to get dinner after the play? Or bagels? I know a pub that serves real New York bagels."

Jule knew she should say no, but she nodded.

"Bagels, good. So for now, let's talk about cheerful things," said Paolo. They brought their drinks in paper cups over to a stand with milk and coffee spoons. "I take two sugars and a giant glug of cream. How do you drink it?"

"With lemon," Jule said. "I need like four slices of lemon for tea."

"Okay, cheerful, distracting things," Paolo said as they walked to a table. "Shall I talk about myself?"

"I don't think anyone could stop you."

He laughed. "When I was eight, I broke my ankle jumping off the roof of my uncle's car. I had a dog named Twister and a hamster named St. George. I wanted to be a detective when I was a boy. I made myself sick from eating too many cherries once. And I haven't been out with anyone since you told me not to call you."

She smiled in spite of herself. "Liar."

"Not one single woman. I'm here tonight with Artie Thatcher."

"The friend of your dad's?"

"The one I'm staying with. He said I hadn't seen London if I hadn't seen the RSC. And you?"

Jule was brought back to reality.

She was here with Forrest.

It had been stupid, unthinkably stupid, to let Paolo derail her.

She had been leaving the theater. But then he'd brushed her cheek with his lips. He had touched her fingers. He noticed her hands and he'd said God, she was pretty. He'd said he wanted to call her every day.

Jule had missed Paolo very much.

But Forrest was here.

They couldn't meet. Paolo must absolutely not see Forrest.

"Listen, I have to—"

Forrest appeared at her elbow. He was languid and slouching. "You found a friend," he said to Jule. He said it as if speaking to a puppy.

They had to leave immediately. Jule stood up. "I'm not feeling well," she said. "I got a head rush. I'm nauseated. Can you take me home?" She grabbed Forrest's wrist and pulled him toward the lobby doors.

"You were fine a minute ago," he said, trailing behind her.

"Great to see you," she called to Paolo. "Goodbye."

She had intended Paolo to stay rooted in his seat, but he got up and followed Jule and Forrest to the door. "I'm

Paolo Vallarta-Bellstone," he said, smiling at Forrest as they walked. "I'm a friend of Imogen's."

"We have to go," Jule said.

"Forrest Smith-Martin," Forrest responded. "You've heard, then?"

"Let's *go*," said Jule. *"Now."*

"Heard what?" said Paolo. He kept pace as Jule pulled Forrest outside.

"Sorry, sorry," Jule said. "Something is wrong with me. Get a taxi. Please."

They were outside now, in heavy rain. The Barbican Centre had long walkways leading to the street. Jule pulled Forrest along the pavement.

Paolo stopped under the shelter of the building, unwilling to get wet.

Jule flagged a black taxi. Got in. Gave the address of the flat in St. John's Wood.

Then she took a deep breath and settled her mind. She decided what to tell Forrest.

"I left my jacket on my seat," he complained. "Are you sick?"

"No, not really."

"Then what was it? Why are we going home?"

"That guy has been bothering me."

"Paolo?"

"Yes. He calls me all the time. Like, many times a day. Texts. Emails. I think he's following me."

"You have weird relationships."

"It's not a relationship. He doesn't take no for an answer. That's why I had to get away."

"Paolo something Bellstone, right?" said Forrest. "That was his name?"

"Yeah."

"Is he related to Stuart Bellstone?"

"I don't know."

"But was that the last name? Bellstone?" Forrest had his phone out. "On Wikipedia it says—yeah, the son of Stuart Bellstone, the D and G trading scandal, blah, blah, his son is Paolo Vallarta-Bellstone."

"I guess so," said Jule. "I think about him as little as I possibly can."

"Bellstone, that's funny," said Forrest. "Did Imogen meet him?"

"Yes. No." She was flustered.

"Which is it?"

"Their families know each other. We ran into him when we first got to London."

"And now he's stalking you?"

"Yes."

"And it never occurred to you that this stalker Bellstone might be worth mentioning to the police in terms of investigating Immie's disappearance?"

"He has nothing to do with anything."

"He might. There are a lot of things that don't add up."

"Immie killed herself and there's nothing more to it," snapped Jule. "She was depressed and she didn't love you anymore and she didn't love me enough to stay alive, either. Stop acting like there's anything else that could have happened."

Forrest bit his lip and they rode in silence. After a minute or two, Jule looked over and saw that he was crying.

In the morning, Forrest was gone. He was simply not on the fold-out couch. His bag was not in the hall closet. His fuzzy man-sweaters were not lying around the room. His laptop was gone and so were his French novels. He had left his dirty dishes in the sink.

Jule wouldn't miss him. She never wanted to see him again. But she didn't want him leaving without saying why.

What had Paolo said to Forrest the night before? Only "I'm a friend of Imogen's" and "Heard what?"—and his name. That was all.

He hadn't heard Paolo call Jule *Imogen*. Had he?

No.

Maybe.

No.

Why did Forrest want Paolo investigated? Did he think Imogen had been stalked and murdered? Did he think Imogen had been romantically involved with Paolo? Did he think Jule was lying?

Jule packed her bags and went to a youth hostel she'd read about, on the other end of town.

15

Eight days before Jule left for the youth hostel, she called Forrest's cell from the London flat. Her hands were shaking. She sat on the kitchen counter next to the bread box and let her feet dangle. It was very early in the morning. She wanted to get this call over with.

"Hey, Jule," he said. "Is Imogen back?"

"No, she's not."

"Oh." There was a pause. "Then why are you calling me?" The disdain in Forrest's voice was palpable.

"I have some bad news," Jule said. "I'm sorry."

"What is it?"

"Where are you?"

"In the newsagent's. Which is apparently what they call newsstands over here."

"You should step outside."

"All right." Jule waited while he walked. "What is it?" Forrest asked.

"I found a note, in the flat. From Imogen."

"What kind of note?"

"It was in the bread box. I'm going to read it." Jule held the note in her fingers. There were the tall, loopy letters of Immie's signature, her typical phrases, and her favorite words.

Hey, Jule. By the time you read this, I'll have taken an overdose of sleeping pills. Then I'll have hailed a taxi to the Westminster Bridge.

I'll have stones in my pockets. Lots of stones. I've been collecting them all week. And I will be drowned. The river will have me and I will feel some relief.

I'm sure you'll wonder why. It's hard to give an answer. Nothing is right. I don't feel at home anywhere. I haven't ever felt at home. I don't think I ever will.

Forrest couldn't understand. Neither could Brooke. But you—I think you can. You know the me that nobody else can love. If there is a me, at all.

Immie

"Oh God. Oh God." Forrest said it over and over.

Jule thought of the beautiful Westminster Bridge with its stone arches and its green railings, and of the heavy, cold river flowing underneath it. She thought of Immie's body, a white shirt floating around her, facedown in the water, in a pool of blood. She really did feel the loss of Imogen Sokoloff acutely, more than Forrest ever could. "She wrote the note days ago," Jule told Forrest when he finally went silent. "She's been gone since Wednesday."

"You said she went to Paris."

"I was guessing."

"Maybe she didn't jump."

"She left a suicide note."

"But why? Why would she?"

"She never felt at home. You know that was true about her. She said it in the note." Jule swallowed and then said what she knew Forrest would want to hear. "What do you think we should do? I don't know what to do. You're the first person I told."

"I'm coming over," said Forrest. "Call the police."

Forrest arrived at the flat two hours later. He looked hollow and disheveled. He brought his bags from the hotel and declared he would sleep on the couch in the den until things were settled. Jule could take the bedroom. Neither of them should be alone, he said.

She didn't want him there. She was feeling sad and vulnerable. With Forrest, she preferred to have her armor on. Still, he was good in a crisis, she gave him that. He set himself to texting and telephoning people, and he talked to everyone with an extreme gentleness Jule hadn't known he possessed. The Sokoloffs, their friends from Martha's Vineyard, Immie's college friends: Forrest got in touch with everyone personally, checking them neatly off a list he'd made.

Jule called the London police. They came in, bustling, while Forrest was on the phone with Patti. The cops took the note in Imogen's handwriting, then asked for statements from Jule and Forrest.

They agreed it didn't look like Immie had gone traveling. Her suitcases were in the closet, as were her clothes. Her wallet and credit cards were in a bag they found. Her laptop wasn't in the flat, however, and her driver's license and passport were missing.

Forrest asked a police officer if the suicide note could be a forgery. "Maybe a kidnapper wanted to put suspicion elsewhere," he said. "Or maybe it was a note she was forced to write? Is there a way you could tell if she was forced to write it?"

"Forrest, the note was in the bread box," Jule reminded him gently. "Immie left it for me in the bread box."

"Why would Miss Sokoloff be kidnapped?" asked the officer.

"Money. Someone could be holding her for ransom. It's strange that her laptop is missing. Or she could have been murdered. Like, by someone who made her write the note."

The officers listened to Forrest's theories. They pointed out that he himself was the most suspicious person: an ex-boyfriend who had recently arrived in the city looking for Imogen. But they also made it clear they didn't really suspect a crime of any kind. They looked for signs of a struggle but found none.

Forrest said Imogen could have been abducted from outside the apartment, but the police officers reminded him about the bread box. "Suicide note makes it clear," they said. They asked if that was Immie's handwriting, and Jule said it was. They asked Forrest, and he said it was, too. Or at least, it looked like it.

Jule gave them Imogen's UK phone. It showed only calls to local museums and emails from her parents, Forrest, Vivian Abromowitz, and a few more friends Jule could identify. The officers asked for Immie's bank records. Jule gave them some papers printed out from the missing computer. They were in a drawer of the desk in the living room.

The officers promised to search the river for Imogen's body, but they also noted that if her body was weighted with stones, it wouldn't surface easily. It had probably been moved away from the Westminster Bridge by the current.

If they found her at all, it might take days or even weeks.

14

Six weeks earlier, Jule arrived in London for the first time. It was the day after Christmas. She took a cab to the hotel she'd booked. The English money was too large to fit neatly into her wallet. The cab was mad expensive, but she didn't care. She was funded.

The hotel was an old and formal building, remodeled inside. A gentleman wearing a checked jacket sat at a desk. He had a record of the reservation and showed Jule to her room personally. He chatted while a porter carried her things. She loved the way he talked, as if he'd stepped out of a Dickens novel.

The walls of the suite were papered in black-and-white toile. Heavy brocade curtains covered the windows. The bathroom had heated floors. The towels were cream-colored and textured with small squares. Lavender soap was wrapped in brown paper.

Jule ordered a steak from room service. When it came, she ate the whole thing and drank two large glasses of water. After that, she slept for eighteen hours.

When she woke, she was elated.

This was a new city and a foreign country, the city of *Vanity Fair* and *Great Expectations*. It was Immie's city, but it would become Jule's own, just as the books Immie loved had become part of Jule, too.

She pushed open the curtains. London stretched out below her. Red buses and beetle-black taxis crawled through traffic on narrow streets. The buildings looked hundreds of years old. She thought of all the lives being led down there, people driving on the left, eating crumpets, drinking tea, watching telly.

Jule was stripped of guilt and sorrow, as if she'd shed a skin. She saw herself as a lone vigilante, a superhero in repose, a spy. She was braver than anyone in the hotel, braver than all of London, braver than ordinary by far.

Back in the summer on Martha's Vineyard, Immie had told Jule about owning a flat in London. She had said, "The keys are right here. We could go tomorrow," and patted her bag.

But she hadn't mentioned it ever again.

Now Jule called the building manager who handled the flat and told him Immie was in town. Could he arrange for cleanup and an airing? Could some groceries be brought in, and fresh flowers? Yes, everything could be arranged.

When the flat was ready, Immie's key turned easily in the lock. The place was a large one-bedroom with a den in St. John's Wood, near lots of shops. It occupied the top floor of a white town house and had windows that looked out onto trees. The cupboards held soft towels and sheets with a ticking stripe. There was only a bathtub, no shower. The fridge was tiny and the kitchen barely furnished. Immie had fixed up the flat before she'd learned to cook. But that didn't matter.

The June after high school graduation, Jule knew, Imogen had attended a summer abroad program in London. While she was there, she bought the flat with encouragement from her financial advisor. The sale had gone through quickly, and Immie and her friends had shopped in the Portobello Road market for antiques and in Harrods for textiles. Immie had covered the front door with instant photographs from that summer—maybe fifty of them. Most featured her and a crew of girls and boys, arms around each other, in front of places like the Tower of London or Madame Tussauds.

Jule put her things away in the flat and then took the photographs down. She threw them in the trash and took the garbage bag down to the basement.

In the weeks that followed, Jule acquired a new laptop and put the two old ones in the incinerator. She went to museums and restaurants, eating steaks in quiet establishments and burgers in noisy pubs. She was charming with servers. She chatted with booksellers and told them Immie's name. She talked to tourists—temporary people—and sometimes went to a meal with them or joined them at the theater. She felt as she imagined Immie would: welcome everywhere. She worked out every day and she ate only food she liked. Other than that, she lived Imogen's life.

At the start of her third week in London, Jule went to Madame Tussauds. The museum is a famous attraction, full of Bollywood actors, members of the royal family, and the dimpled stars of boy bands, all sculpted in wax. The place was crowded with loud American children and their aggravated parents.

Jule was looking at the wax model of Charles Dickens, who sat morosely in a hard wooden chair, when someone spoke to her.

"If he lived now," said Paolo Vallarta-Bellstone, "he'd have shaved that baldy head."

"If he lived now," said Jule, "he'd be a TV writer."

"Do you remember me?" he asked. "I'm Paolo. We met in the summer on Martha's Vineyard." He had a bashful grin. He was wearing old jeans and a soft orange T-shirt. Beat-up Vans. He'd been backpacking, Jule knew. "You changed your hair," he added. "I wasn't sure it was you, at first."

He looked good. Jule had forgotten how good he looked. She had kissed him once. His thick black hair was in his face. His cheeks looked slightly sunburnt and his lips a bit chapped. Maybe he'd been skiing.

"I remember you," she said. "You can't decide between butterscotch and hot fudge, you get sick on carousels, you might want to be a doctor someday. You actually play golf, which is stodgy; you're traveling the world, which is interesting; you follow girls around museums and sneak up on them when they stop to look at a famous novelist made of wax."

"I'm just gonna say thank you," said Paolo, "even though you made mean remarks about golf. I'm glad you remember me. Have you read him?" He pointed at Dickens. "I was supposed to in school, but I blew it off."

"Yeah."

"What's the best one, you think?"

"Great Expectations."

"What's it about?" Paolo wasn't looking at the waxwork. He was looking at Jule, intently. He reached out and ran his hand down her arm while she answered. It was a very confident move, to touch her like that, seconds after reintroducing himself. She didn't usually let people touch her, but she didn't mind with Paolo. He was very gentle.

"This orphan boy falls in love with a rich girl," she told

him. "Her name is Estella. And Estella has been trained her whole life to break men's hearts, and perhaps she has no heart of her own. She was brought up by a crazy lady who was jilted at the altar."

"So this Estella breaks the boy's heart?"

"Many times over. On purpose. Estella doesn't know how to do anything else. Breaking hearts is her only power in the world." They walked away from Dickens and into a different section of the museum. "Are you here on your own?" Jule asked.

"With a friend of my dad's. I've been staying with him for a few days. He wants to show me the city, only he keeps having to sit down. Artie Thatcher, you know him?"

"No."

"His sciatica flared. He went to rest in the tea shop."

"And how come you're in London?"

"I did the backpacking thing through Spain, Portugal, France, Germany, the Netherlands, France again. Then I came here. I was traveling with my friend, but he went home for Christmas, and I didn't feel like going back, so I came to stay with Artie for the holidays. You?"

"I have a flat here."

Paolo leaned in close and pointed down a dark hall. "Hey, there's the Chamber of Horrors, down that hall. Will you go in there with me? I need protection."

"From what?"

"From the crazy-scary waxworks, that's what," Paolo said. "It's going to be a prison with escaped inmates. I looked it up. Lots of blood and guts."

"And you want to go?"

"I love blood and guts. But not alone." He smiled. "Are you coming to protect me from the inmates of the asylum, Imogen?" They stood at the door to the Chamber of Horrors now.

"Sure," said Jule. "I'll protect you."

There had never been three boyfriends at Stanford.

There had never been three boyfriends anywhere. Or even one boyfriend.

Jule didn't need a guy, wasn't sure she liked guys, wasn't sure she liked *anyone*.

She was supposed to meet Paolo at eight o'clock. She brushed her teeth three times and changed her clothes twice. She put on jasmine perfume.

When she spotted him waiting by the carousel where they had arranged to meet, she nearly turned around and left. Paolo was watching a street performer. He had his scarf wrapped tightly against the January wind.

Jule told herself she shouldn't get close to people. No one was worth the risk. She would leave right now, she was about to leave—but then Paolo saw her and ran at her, top speed, like a little boy, stopping short before he crashed. He swung her around by the wrists and said, "Jeez, it's like a movie. Can you believe we're in London? Everything we know is on the other side of the ocean."

And he was right. Everything was on the other side of the ocean.

Tonight would be okay.

Paolo took Jule walking along the Thames. Street performers played accordions and walked low tightropes. The two of them poked around in a bookshop for a while, and then Jule bought them both cotton candy. Folding sweet pink clouds into their mouths, they walked along to the Westminster Bridge.

Paolo took Jule's hand and she let him. He rubbed her wrist softly now and then with the pad of his thumb. It sent a warm thrill up her arm. She was surprised that his touch could feel so comforting.

The Westminster Bridge was a series of stone arches over the river, gray and green. Light from the lamps on top of the bridge shone onto the rushing river.

"The worst thing in that Chamber of Horrors was Jack the Ripper," said Paolo. "Know why?"

"Why?"

"One, because he was never caught. And two, because there's a rumor that he killed himself by jumping off this exact bridge."

"Get out."

"He did. He was probably standing right here when he jumped. I read it on the Internet."

"That is complete trash," said Jule. "No one even knows who Jack the Ripper really was."

"You're right," he said. "It is trash."

He kissed her then, under the streetlight. Like a scene from a film. The stones were damp in the fog and glistened. Their coats flapped in the wind. Jule shivered in the night air, and Paolo put his warm hand against her neck.

He kissed like he couldn't imagine wanting to be anywhere else on the planet, because wasn't this so nice, and didn't this feel good? As if he knew she didn't let people touch her, and he knew she would let *him* touch her, and he was the luckiest guy in the world. Jule felt as if the river underneath her were running through her veins.

She wanted to be herself with him.

Wondered if she *was* being herself. If she could go on being herself.

And if anyone could love the person she was.

They pulled apart and walked in silence for a minute. A crowd of four drunk young women headed toward them, crossing the bridge precariously on high heels. "I can't believe they made us leave," one of them complained, slurring her words.

"They should want our business, those buggers," said another. Their accents were Yorkshire.

"Ooh, he's cute." The first one looked at Paolo from ten feet away.

"You think he wants to go get a drink?"

"Ha! Cheeky."

"I dunno. Ask him."

One woman called out, "If you want a night out, good sir, you can come along with us."

Paolo blushed. "What?"

"Are you coming?" she asked. "Just you."

Paolo shook his head. The women walked away, giggling, and he watched them until they were off the bridge. Then he took Jule's hand again.

The mood was different, though. They no longer knew what to say to each other.

Finally, Paolo said: "Did you know Brooke Lannon?"

What?

Imogen's friend Brooke. What did Paolo have to do with Brooke?

Jule made her voice light. "Yeah, from Vassar. How come?"

"Brooke—she passed away about a week ago." Paolo looked at the ground.

"What? Oh no."

"I didn't mean to be the one to tell you. I didn't put it together that you'd know her till now," said Paolo. "And then it popped out."

"How do you know Brooke?"

"I don't, really. She was friends with my sister from summer camp."

"What happened?" Jule wanted to hear his answer, desperately, but she calmed her voice.

"It was an accident. She was up in a park north of San Francisco. She was there visiting some friends who went to college in the city, but they were busy or something, and Brooke went hiking. It was a day hike, but late, when it was getting dark. She was on a nature preserve by herself. And she just—she fell off this walkway. A walkway over a ravine."

"She fell?"

"They think she'd been drinking. She hit her head and nobody found her till this morning. Except some animals. The body was pretty messed up."

Jule shivered. She thought of Brooke Lannon, with her loud, show-off laugh. Brooke, who drank too much. Brooke, with that perverse streak of humor, the sleek yellow hair and seal-like body. The entitled set of her jaw. Silly, petty, harsh Brooke. "How do they know what happened?"

"She tipped herself over the railing. Maybe climbing up to see something. They found her car in the lot with an empty vodka bottle in it."

"Was it suicide?"

"No, no. Just an accident. It was in the news today, like a cautionary tale. You know, always take a buddy when you go out in nature. Don't drink vodka and then hike across a ravine. Her family got worried when she didn't come home for Christmas Eve, but the police assumed she'd just gone deliberately missing."

Jule felt cold and strange. She hadn't thought of Brooke since she'd gotten to London. She could have looked her up online, but she hadn't. She had cut Brooke out completely. "You're sure it was an accident?"

"A terrible accident," said Paolo. "I'm so sorry."

They walked for a ways in awkward silence.

Paolo pulled his hat down over his ears.

After a minute, Jule reached over and took his hand again. She wanted to touch him. Admitting that and doing it felt more like an act of bravery than any fight she had ever been in. "Let's not think about it," she said. "Let's be on the other side of the ocean and feel lucky."

She let him walk her home, and he kissed her again in front of her building. They huddled together on the steps to keep warm as merry snowflakes drifted through the air.

Early the next day, Paolo showed up at the flat carrying a tote bag. Jule was wearing pajama pants and a camisole when he rang the buzzer. She made him wait in the hall until she put clothes on.

"I'm borrowing my friend's house in Dorset," he said, following her to the kitchen. "And I rented a car. Everything else anyone could possibly need for a weekend away is in this bag."

Jule peered into the sack he held out: four Crunchie bars, Hula Hoops, Swedish Fish, two bottles of seltzer, and a bag of salt and vinegar potato chips. "You don't have any clothes in there. Or even a toothbrush."

"Those are for amateurs."

She laughed. "Ew."

"Okay, fine, I have my backpack in the car. But these are the important items," Paolo said. "We can see Stonehenge on the way. Have you seen it?"

"No." Jule was indeed particularly curious to see Stonehenge, which she'd read about in a Thomas Hardy novel she'd bought in a San Francisco bookshop, but she wanted to see *all the things*—that was how she felt. All of London she hadn't yet seen, all of England, all of the great wide world— and to feel free, powerful, and yes, entitled, to witness and understand what was out there.

"It'll have ancient mystery, so that'll be good," said Paolo. "Then when we get to the house, we can hike around and look at sheep in meadows. Or take pictures of sheep. Maybe pat them. Whatever people do in the countryside."

"Are you inviting me?"

"Yes! There will be separate bedrooms. Available."

He perched himself on the edge of her kitchen chair, as if unsure of his welcome. As if maybe he'd been too forward.

"You're nervous right now," she said, stalling for time.

She wanted to say yes. She knew she shouldn't.

"Yeah, I'm very nervous."

"Why?"

Paolo thought for a moment. "The stakes are higher now. It matters to me what your answer is." He stood up slowly and kissed the side of her neck. She leaned into him, and he was shaking a little. She kissed his soft earlobe and then his lips, standing on tiptoe there in the kitchen.

"Is that a yes?" he whispered.

Jule knew she shouldn't go.

It was the worst idea. She had left this possibility behind long ago. Love was what you gave up when you became— whatever she was now. Larger than life. Dangerous. She had taken risks and reinvented herself.

Now this boy was in her kitchen, trembling when he kissed her, holding a bag of junk food and fizzy water. Talking nonsense about sheep.

Jule crossed to the other side of the room and washed her hands in the sink. She felt as if the universe was offering her something beautiful and special. It wouldn't come around again with another such offer.

Paolo walked over and put his hand on her shoulder, very, very gently, as if asking permission. As if in awe that he was allowed to touch her.

And Jule turned around and told him yes.

Stonehenge was closed.

And it was raining.

You couldn't get close to the actual stones unless you'd bought tickets ahead of time. Jule and Paolo could see some big rocks in the distance as they drove up, but from the visitors' center, nothing.

"I promised you ancient mystery, and now it's nothing but a parking lot," said Paolo, half sad and half joking, as they got back in the car. "I should have looked it up."

"That's all right."

"I do know how to work the Internet."

"Oh, don't worry. I'm more excited about the sheep anyway."

He smiled. "Are you really?"

"Sure. Can you guarantee sheep?"

"Are you serious? Because I don't think I *can* actually guarantee sheep, and I don't want to let you down again."

"No. I don't care about sheep at all."

Paolo shook his head. "I should have known. Sheep are not Stonehenge. We have to face that. Even the very best sheep are never going to be Stonehenge."

"Let's eat the Swedish Fish," she said, to cheer him up.

"Perfect," said Paolo. "That is a perfect plan."

The house wasn't a house at all. It was a mansion. A great house, built in the nineteenth century. It had grounds and a gated entryway. Paolo had a code for the gate. He punched it in and drove along a curving driveway.

The walls were brick and covered with ivy. On one side, there was a sloping garden of rosebushes and stone benches, ending at a round gazebo by the edge of a stream.

Paolo fumbled in his pockets. "I have the keys in here somewhere."

It was raining hard now. They stood in the doorway, holding their bags.

"Damn, where are they?" Paolo patted his jacket, his pants, his jacket again. "Keys, keys." He looked in the tote bag. Looked in his backpack. Ran out and looked in the car.

He sat down in the doorway, under cover from the rain, and pulled everything out of all his pockets. Then everything out of the tote bag. And everything out of the backpack.

"You don't have the keys," Jule said.

"I don't have the keys."

He was a con artist, a hustler. He wasn't Paolo Vallarta-Bellstone at all. What proof had Jule seen? No ID, no online photos. Just what he told her, his manner, his knowledge of Imogen's family. "Are you really friends with these people?" she asked, making her voice light.

"It's my friend Nigel's family's country house. He had me here in the summer as a guest, and no one is using it, and—I knew the gate code, didn't I?"

"I'm not actually doubting you," she lied.

"We can go around the back and see if the kitchen door is open. There's a kitchen garden, from—from whenever in history they had kitchen gardens," said Paolo. "I think the technical term is ye olden days."

They pulled their jackets over their heads and ran through the rain, stepping in puddles and laughing.

Paolo jiggled the kitchen door. It was locked. He wandered around, looking under rocks for a spare key, while Jule huddled under the umbrella.

She pulled out her phone and searched his name, looking for images.

Phew. He was definitely Paolo Vallarta-Bellstone. There were photographs of him at charity fund-raisers, standing next to his parents, wearing no tie at an event where clearly men were supposed to wear ties. Pictures of him with other guys on a soccer field. A high school graduation photo that showed a mouth full of braces and a bad haircut, posted by a grandmother who had blogged a total of three times.

Jule *was* glad he was Paolo and not some hustler. She liked what a good person he was. It was better that he was genuine because she could believe in him. But there was so much of Paolo that Jule would never know. So much history he'd never get to tell her.

Paolo gave up hunting for the key. His hair was soaked. "The windows are alarmed," he said. "I think it's hopeless."

"What should we do?"

"We better go in the gazebo and kiss for a while," said Paolo.

The rain didn't let up.

They drove in damp clothes toward London and stopped at a pub to eat fried food.

Paolo pulled the car up to Jule's building. He didn't kiss her but reached his hand out to hold hers. "I like you," he said. "I thought—I guess I made that clear already? But I thought I should say it."

Jule liked him back. She liked herself with him.

But she wasn't herself with him. She didn't know what it was, or even who it was, that Paolo liked.

Could be Immie. Could be Jule.

She wasn't sure where to draw the line between them anymore. Jule smelled of jasmine like Imogen, Jule spoke like Imogen, Jule loved the books Immie loved. Those things were true. Jule was an orphan like Immie, a self-created person, a person with a mysterious past. So much of Imogen was in Jule, she felt, and so much of Jule was in Imogen.

But Paolo thought Patti and Gil were her parents. He thought she'd been to college with poor dead Brooke Lannon. He thought she was Jewish and rich and owned a London flat. Those lies were part of what he liked. It was impossible to tell him the truth, and even if she did, he'd hate her for the lie.

"I can't see you," she told him.

"What?"

"I can't see you. Like this. At all."

"Why not?"

"I just can't."

"Is there someone else? That you're going out with? I could take a number or get in line or something."

"No. Yes. No."

"Which is it? Can I change your mind?"

"I'm not available." She could tell him she had someone else, but she didn't want to lie to him anymore.

"Why not?"

She opened the car door. "I have no heart."

"Wait."

"No."

"Please wait."

"I have to go."

"Did you have a bad time? I mean, aside from the rain, no Stonehenge, no country house, no sheep? Aside from the fact that it was a day of disaster upon disaster?"

Jule wanted to stay in the car. To touch his lips with her fingertips and to relax into being Immie and to let the lies build up on each other.

But it would not do.

"Leave me the fuck alone, Paolo," she snapped. She pushed open the car door and stepped into the downpour.

A couple of weeks went by. Jule kept her eyebrows plucked thin. She bought clothes and more clothes, lovely things with fat price tags. She bought cookbooks for the flat's kitchen, though she never used them. She went to the ballet, to the opera, to the theater. She saw all the things, historic sites and museums and famous buildings. She bought antiques on Portobello Road.

Late one night, Forrest showed up at the flat. He was supposed to be in America.

Jule forced down panic as she looked through the peephole. She wanted to open the window and climb the drainpipe to the roof, leap onto the next building, and, frankly, just not be home. She wanted to change her eyebrows and her hair and her makeup and—

He rang the buzzer a second time. Jule settled on taking off her rings and putting on joggers and a T-shirt instead of the maxi dress she'd been wearing. She stood before the door and reminded herself that she had always known Forrest might show up. It was Immie's flat. She had a strategy. She could handle him. She unlocked the door.

"Forrest. What a great surprise."

"Jule."

"You look tired. Are you okay? Come in."

He was holding a weekender bag. She took it from him and brought it into the flat.

"I just got off a plane," said Forrest, rubbing his jaw and squinting through his glasses.

"Did you take a cab from Heathrow?"

"Yes." He eyed her coldly. "Why are *you* here? In Imogen's apartment?"

"I'm staying here for a bit. She gave me her keys."

"Where is she? I want to see her."

"She didn't come back last night. How did you find the flat?"

"Mrs. Sokoloff gave me the address." Forrest looked down at the floor, awkward. "It was a long flight. Could I have a glass of water?"

Jule led the way into the kitchen. She gave him water from the tap with no ice. She had lemons in a bowl on the counter, because they fit her idea of how the flat should look, but inside the cupboards and the fridge, there was nothing Imogen would have stocked. Jule ate saltines and sugary peanut butter, packets of salami and chocolate bars. She hoped Forrest wouldn't ask for food.

"Where is Immie, again?" he asked.

"I told you, she isn't here."

"But, Jule." He grabbed her arm, and for a moment she was afraid of him, afraid of his hard hands pressing the fabric of her shirt, thin and weak as he was. "Where is she instead of here?" He spoke very slowly. She hated the feel of his body close to hers.

"Don't you ever fucking touch me," she told him. "Ever. You understand?"

He let her arm drop and walked into the living room, where he draped himself on the couch without being invited. "I think you know where she is. That's all."

"She probably went to Paris for the weekend. You can go really quickly from here through the Chunnel."

"Paris?"

"I'm guessing."

"Did she tell you not to tell me where she went?"

"No. We didn't even know you were coming."

Forrest sank back in his seat. "I need to see her. I texted her, but she might have blocked me."

"She got a UK phone, with a different number."

"She doesn't answer my emails, either. That's why I came all the way here. I was hoping to talk to her."

Jule made them some tea while Forrest phoned hotels. He had to make twelve calls before he found one with a room he could book for a few nights.

He'd been arrogant enough to think Imogen would let him stay.

13

Two days before she would arrive in London, Jule was on foot, trudging up a San Francisco hill with a heavy statue of a lion in her backpack.

She adored San Francisco. It looked like Immie had said it would, hilly and quaint, yet expansive and elegant. Today Jule had been to see the Asian Art Museum's ceramics exhibit. Her apartment's owner had recommended it.

Maddie Chung, the owner, was spare, fiftyish, and gay. She wore jeans and smoked on the porch and owned a small bookstore. Jule paid in cash by the week for the apartment, which was the top floor of a Victorian house. Maddie and her wife lived in the bottom two stories. She was always talking to Jule about art history and gallery exhibits. She was very kind and seemed to view Jule as in need of goodwill.

Today, when Jule got home, Brooke Lannon was sitting on the steps. Immie's friend from Vassar. "I got here early," said Brooke. "Whatever."

Brooke's convertible had been parked in front of the

building overnight. She needed to come pick it up, but Jule had texted her to please stay and talk.

Brooke had thick thighs, a square jaw, and sleek blond hair that always looked the same. White skin and nude lipstick. A jock style. She'd grown up in La Jolla. She drank too much, played field hockey in high school, and had had a series of boyfriends and one girlfriend, but never love. These were all things Jule knew about her from Martha's Vineyard.

Now Brooke stood up and nearly lost her balance.

"You okay?" Jule asked.

"Not really."

"Have you been drinking?"

"Yes," said Brooke. "What of it?"

Night was falling.

"Let's go for a drive," said Jule. "We can talk."

"A drive?"

"It'll be nice. You have such a cute car. Let me have the keys." The car was the type of thing older men buy to convince themselves they're still sexy. The two seats were camel-colored, the body curved and bright green. Jule wondered if it belonged to Brooke's dad. "I can't have you drive if you've been drinking."

"What are you, the police?"

"Hardly."

"A spy?"

"Brooke."

"Seriously, are you?"

"I can't answer that."

"Ha. That's what a spy would say."

It didn't matter what Jule said or did not say to Brooke

anymore. "Let's go on a hike," said Jule. "I know a place in the state park. We can drive across the Golden Gate Bridge and it'll be mad scenic."

Brooke jangled her car keys in her pocket. "It's kinda late."

"Look," Jule said, "we've had a misunderstanding about Immie, and I'm glad you came over. Let's just go somewhere neutral and talk it out. My apartment is not the best place."

"I don't know if I want to talk to you."

"You showed up early," said Jule. "You want to talk to me."

"Okay, we'll talk it out, hug it out, all that," said Brooke. "It'll make Immie happy." She handed over the keys.

People were stupid when they drank.

Two days before Christmas it was too cold for the convertible, but the top of Brooke's car was down anyway. Brooke insisted. Jule wore jeans, boots, and a warm wool sweater. Her backpack was in the trunk, and in it were her wallet, a second sweater and a clean T-shirt, a wide-mouth water bottle, a packet of baby wipes, a black garbage bag, and the lion statue.

Brooke took a half-empty bottle of vodka out of her shoulder bag but didn't actually drink from it. She went to sleep almost immediately.

Jule drove up through the city. By the time they got to the Golden Gate Bridge, she was antsy. The quiet drive was unnerving. She nudged Brooke awake. "The bridge," she said. "Look." It loomed above them, orange and majestic.

"People love to kill themselves on this bridge," said Brooke thickly.

"What?"

"It's the second most popular suicide bridge in the world," said Brooke. "I read it somewhere."

"What's the first?"

"A bridge on the Yangtze River. I forget the name. I read up on stuff like that," said Brooke. "People think it's poetic, to jump off a bridge. That's why they do it. Whereas, let's say, killing yourself by bleeding out in a bathtub, that's just messy. What are you supposed to wear to bleed out in a bathtub?"

"You don't wear anything."

"How do you know?"

"I just know." Jule wished she hadn't engaged Brooke on this topic.

"I don't want people to see me naked when I'm dead!" yelled Brooke into the air beneath the Golden Gate Bridge. "But I don't want to wear clothes in the bathtub, either! It's very awkward!"

Jule ignored her.

"Anyway, they're building a barrier now, so people can't jump," Brooke went on. "Here on the Golden Gate."

They drove off the bridge in silence and turned toward the park.

Eventually Brooke added: "I shouldn't have brought that up. I don't want to give you ideas."

"I don't have ideas."

"Don't kill yourself," said Brooke.

"I'm not killing myself."

"I'm being your friend right now, okay? Something is not normal with you."

Jule didn't answer.

"I grew up with very normal, stable people," Brooke continued. "We acted normal all day long in my family. So normal I wanted to stab my eyes out. So I'm like an expert. And *you*? You are not normal. You should think about getting help for it, is what I'm saying."

"You think normal is having a shit-ton of money."

"No I don't. Vivian Abromowitz is on full scholarship at Vassar and she's normal, that witch."

"You think it's normal to get what you want all the time," said Jule. "For things to be easy. But it isn't. Most people don't get what they want, like, *ever*. They have doors shut in their faces. They have to strive, all the time. They don't live in your magical land of two-seater cars and perfect teeth and traveling to Italy and fur coats."

"There," said Brooke. "You proved my point."

"How?"

"It's not even normal to say stuff like that. You walked back into Immie's life after not seeing her for years, and within days you've moved into her house, you're borrowing her stuff, you're swimming in her effing pool and letting her pay for your haircuts. You went to freaking Stanford, and boo-hoo, you lost your scholarship, but don't make out like you're some voice of the effing ninety-nine percent. Nobody is shutting any doors on you, Jule. Also, no one wears fur coats because, hello, that's not even ethical. I mean, maybe someone's grandma would, but not a regular person. And I have never said jack about your teeth. Sheesh. You need to learn how to relax and be a human being if you want to have any actual friends and not just people who tolerate you."

Neither of them said anything for the rest of the drive.

They parked and Jule got her backpack from the trunk. She took the gloves out of her jeans pocket and put them on. "Let's leave our phones in the trunk," she said.

Brooke looked at her for a long minute. "Yeah, fine. We're getting our nature on," she said, slurring her speech. They locked up the phones and Jule pocketed the car keys. They checked the sign on the edge of the parking lot. Hiking trails were marked in several colors.

"Let's go to the lookout," Jule said, pointing to the trail marked in blue. "I've been there before."

"Whatever," said Brooke.

It was a four-mile hike round-trip. The park was nearly empty because of the cold and the Christmas season, but a few families were leaving as the day came to a close. Tired kids were whining or being carried. Once Brooke and Jule began heading uphill, the path was empty.

Jule felt her pulse increase. She led the way.

"You have a thing for Imogen," said Brooke, breaking the silence. "Don't think that makes you special. *Everyone* has a thing for Imogen."

"She's my best friend. That's not the same as having a thing," said Jule.

"She's no one's best friend. She's a heartbreaker."

"Don't be mean about her. You're just mad she hasn't texted you."

"She *has* texted me. That's not the point," said Brooke. "Listen. When we made friends freshman year, Immie was in my dorm room all the time: in the morning, bringing me a latte before class; dragging me out to movies the film department was screening; wanting to borrow earrings; bringing me Goldfish crackers because she knew I liked them."

Jule didn't say anything.

Immie had dragged her out to movies. Immie had bought her chocolate. Immie had brought her coffee in bed, when they lived together.

Brooke went on: "She'd come by every Tuesday and Thursday because we had this early-morning Italian class. And at first, I wouldn't even be awake. She'd have to wait while I got clothes on. My roommate bitched because Immie was in there so early, so I started setting my phone. I'd get up and be standing outside the door before Imogen got there.

"And then one day, she didn't come. It was early November, I think. And you know what? She never came again after that. She never brought me a latte or dragged me to the movies. She'd switched over to Vivian Abromowitz. And you know what? I could have been all grade-school about it, Jule. I could have gotten huffy and acted like, ooh, poor me because you can't have two best friends and wah, wah, wah. But I didn't. I was nice to the two of them. And we were all friends. And it was fine."

"Okay."

Jule hated this story. She hated, too, how she had never understood before that the reason Vivian and Brooke disliked each other was Imogen herself.

Brooke went on: "What I'm saying is, Imogen broke Vivian's little heart, too. Later. And Isaac Tupperman's. She led all these different guys on when she was going out with Isaac, and Isaac, of course, got all jealous and insecure. Then

Immie was surprised when he broke up with her—but what did she expect, when she hooked up with other guys? She wanted to see if people would lose their cool and obsess over her. And you know what? That is exactly what you've done, and exactly what a lot of people did in college. That's something Imogen likes, because it makes her feel awesome and sexy, but then you don't get to be friends any longer. The other way to handle it is, you prove yourself a bigger person. Imogen knows you're as strong as she is, or maybe even stronger. Then she respects you, and you go on together."

Jule was silent. This was a new version of the Isaac Tupperman story, Isaac of the Bronx, Coates and Morrison, the poems left on Imogen's bicycle, the possible pregnancy. Hadn't Immie looked up at him with wide eyes? She'd been infatuated and then disillusioned—but only after he'd dumped her. It didn't seem possible she had stepped out on him.

Then, suddenly, it did seem possible. It seemed obvious to Jule now that Imogen—who had felt shallow and second-rate next to Tupperman's intellect and masculinity—would have made herself feel stronger and more powerful than he was by betraying him.

They kept walking through the woods. The sun began to set.

There was no one else on the path.

"You want to be like Immie, then be like her. Fine," Brooke said. They had reached a walkway over a ravine. It led to wooden steps built up to a lookout tower that gave a view of the deep valley and the surrounding hillsides. "But you're not Imogen, you understand?"

"I know I'm not Imogen."

"I'm not sure you do," said Brooke.

"None of that is your business."

"Maybe I've made it my business. Maybe I think you're unstable and the best thing would be for you to back away from Immie and get some help for your mental problems."

"Tell me this. Why are we out here?" asked Jule. She stood on the steps above Brooke.

Below them was the ravine.

The sun was nearly down.

"Why are we out here, I asked," Jule said. She said it lightly, swinging her backpack off her shoulder and opening it as if to get out her water bottle.

"We're going to talk it out, like you said. I want you to stop dicking around with Immie's life, living off her trust fund, making her ignore her friends, and whatever else you're doing."

"I asked you why we're out here," said Jule, bent over her backpack.

Brooke shrugged. "Here exactly? In this park? You drove us here."

"Right."

Jule hefted the bag that held the lion statue from the Asian Art Museum. She swung once, hard, coming down on Brooke's forehead with a horrid crack.

The statue didn't break.

Brooke's head snapped back. She stumbled on the wooden walkway.

Jule moved forward and hit her again. This time from the side. Blood spurted from Brooke's head. It splattered across Jule's face.

Brooke collapsed against the railing, her hands clutching the wooden bars.

Jule dropped the statue and went at Brooke low. She grabbed her around the knees. Brooke kicked out and hit Jule in the shoulder, scrabbling with her hands to regain her grip on the railing. She kicked hard, and Jule's shoulder popped out, dislocating with a jolt of pain.

Fuck.

Jule's vision went white for a minute. She lost hold of Brooke, and with her left arm hanging lame, locked her right arm and slammed it up under Brooke's forearms, making Brooke let go of the railing. Then she bent over and went in low again. She got Brooke's legs, which scrabbled on the ground, grabbed them, got her good shoulder underneath Brooke's body, and lurched her up and over.

Everything was still.

Brooke's silken blond hair plummeted.

There was a dull crack as her body hit the tops of the

trees, and another as she landed at the bottom of the rocky ravine.

Jule leaned over the railing. The body was invisible beneath the green.

She looked around. Still no one on the path.

Her shoulder was dislocated. It hurt so much she couldn't think straight.

She hadn't bargained on an injury. If she couldn't move her dislocated arm, she was going to fail, because Brooke was dead and her blood was everywhere and Jule had to change clothes. Now.

Jule forced herself to calm her breathing. Forced her eyes to focus.

Holding her left wrist with her right hand, she lifted the left arm up in a J-movement, pulling away from the body. Once, twice—God, it hurt—but on the third try, the left shoulder popped back in.

The pain disappeared.

Jule had seen a guy do that once, in a martial arts gym. She had asked him about it.

All right, then. She looked down at her sweater. It was splattered with blood. She pulled it off. The shirt underneath was wet, too. She yanked her shirt off and used a clean corner of it to wipe her hands and face. She pulled off her gloves. She took the baby wipes from the backpack and cleaned herself up—chest, arms, neck, hands—shivering in the winter air. She shoved the bloody clothes and wipes into the black garbage bag, tied it shut, and tucked everything into the backpack.

She put on the clean shirt and the clean sweater.

There was blood on the bag that held the statue.

Jule pulled that bag off and turned it inside out so the blood was inside. She put the statue in her backpack and stuffed the dirty bag into her wide-mouth water bottle.

She used the wipes to take spots of blood off the walkway, then stuffed all her trash into the water bottle, too.

She looked around.

The path was empty.

Jule touched her shoulder gingerly. It was okay. She washed her face, ears, and hair four more times with wipes, wishing she'd remembered to bring a compact mirror. She looked over the edge of the bridge, into the ravine.

She could not see Brooke.

She hiked back out along the trail. She felt she could walk forever and never get tired. She saw no one on the path until near the entrance, where she passed four sporty guys wearing Santa hats and holding flashlights, starting up the trail marked in yellow.

At the car, Jule paused.

It should stay here. If she drove it anywhere, it wouldn't make sense when people found Brooke's body in the ravine.

Carefully, she got inside. She took out the wipes and began to rub down the emergency brake, then stopped.

No, no. That was the wrong plan. Why hadn't she thought it through before? It would look bad if there were zero prints in the car. Brooke's prints *should* be there. It would seem odd, now that the brake was clean.

Think. Think. The bottle of vodka lay on the floor of the passenger seat. Jule picked it up with a wipe and unscrewed the cap. Then she poured some of the vodka onto the brake, as if it had spilled accidentally. Maybe that would make it seem legit that there were no prints there. She had no idea if crime scene investigators looked at that sort of thing. She didn't know what they looked at, actually.

Damn.

She got out of the car. She forced herself to think logically. Her own prints weren't on file anywhere. She had no criminal record. Police *would* be able to tell that someone else had driven the car, if they looked—but they wouldn't know it was Jule.

There was no evidence that anyone named Jule West Williams had ever lived in or visited the city of San Francisco.

She popped the trunk and took Brooke's phone out, as well as her own. Then, still shaking, she locked the car and walked away.

It was a cold night. Jule walked quickly to stay warm. A mile on foot from the park and she was feeling calmer. She dumped the water bottle into a trash can by the side of the road. Farther down, she tossed the bloody clothes in their black plastic bag deep into a dumpster.

Then she kept walking.

The Golden Gate Bridge was ablaze against the night sky. Jule was small beneath it but felt as if a spotlight shone on her from above. She hurled Brooke's car keys and phone out over the side of the bridge and into the water.

Her life was cinematic. She looked superb in the light from the streetlamps. After the fight, her cheeks were flushed. Bruises were forming underneath her clothes, but her hair looked excellent. And oh, her clothes were so very flattering. Yes, it was true that she was criminally violent. Brutal, even.

But that was her job and she was uniquely qualified for it, so it was sexy.

The moon was a crescent and the wind harsh. Jule sucked in big lungfuls of air and breathed the glamour and pain and beauty of the action-hero life.

Back in the apartment, she took the lion statue out of her backpack and poured bleach on it. Then she ran the shower on it, dried it, and placed it on the mantel.

Imogen would have liked that statue. She loved cats.

Jule bought a plane ticket to London that left from Portland, Oregon, under Imogen's name. Then she got a taxi to the bus station.

Arriving, she realized she had just missed the nine p.m. bus. The next bus wasn't until seven in the morning.

As Jule settled down to wait, the adrenaline high of the past few hours seeped away. She bought three packs of peanut M&Ms from a vending machine and sat on top of her bags. Suddenly she was exhausted and afraid.

There were only a couple of other people in the room, all of them using the station for a night's shelter. Jule sucked on the M&Ms to make them last. She tried to read, but she couldn't concentrate. After twenty-five minutes, a drunk man sleeping on a bench woke up and began to sing loudly:

> *"God rest ye merry, gentlemen,*
> *Let nothing you dismay*
> *Remember, Christ, our savior,*
> *Was born on Christmas Day,*
> *To save us all from Satan's power*
> *When we had gone astray."*

Jule knew she had gone way fucking astray. She had killed a stupid loudmouth girl with brutal premeditation. There would never be a savior who could rescue her from whatever had made her do it. She had never had a savior.

That was it. No going back. She was alone in a bone-cold

bus station on December 23, listening to a drunk guy and scraping the last of someone's blood from underneath her nails with the corner of her bus ticket. Other people, good people, were baking gingerbread cookies, eating peppermints, and tying bows on holiday gifts. They were quarreling and decorating and cleaning up after big meals, tipsy from mulled wine, watching uplifting old movies.

Jule was here. She deserved the chill, the loneliness, the drunks and the trash, a thousand worse punishments and tortures.

The clock went around the dial. It hit midnight and became, officially, Christmas Eve. Jule bought a hot chocolate from a machine.

She drank it and felt warmer. She talked herself up from despair. After all, she was brave, smart, and strong. She had done the deed with credible efficiency. With style, even. She had committed murder with an effing kitty-cat statue in a beautiful state park over a massive and scenic ravine. There had not been a single witness. She had left no blood anywhere.

Killing Brooke had been self-protection.

People needed to protect themselves. It was human nature, and Jule had spent years training to make herself especially good at it. The events of today were proof that she was even more capable than she'd hoped. She was phenomenal, in fact—a fighting mutant, a supercreature. Fucking Wolverine didn't stop to mourn the people his claws went through. He killed people all the time in self-defense, or for a worthy cause. Same with Bourne, Bond, and the rest of them. Heroes didn't wish for gingerbread, presents, and peppermint. Jule would not, either. It wasn't like she'd ever had them anyway. There was nothing to mope about.

> *"God rest ye merry, gentlemen,*
> *Let nothing you dismay . . ."*

The drunk started up again.

"Shut up before I come over there and make you!" Jule yelled at him.

The singing stopped.

She tipped the last of the chocolate into her mouth. She wouldn't think about going astray. She wouldn't feel guilty. She would follow this action-hero path and power on.

Jule West Williams spent December 24 on a nineteen-hour bus ride and fell asleep early Christmas morning in a Portland, Oregon, airport hotel. At eleven a.m., she shuttled to the airport and checked her bags for the night flight to London, business class. She ate a burger in the food court. She bought books and sprayed herself with unfamiliar perfume in duty-free.

12

The day before the hike, Jule had a call from Brooke. "Where are you?" Brooke barked, without saying hello. "Have you seen Immie?"

"No." Jule had just finished a workout. She sat down on a bench outside Haight-Ashbury Fitness.

"I've sent her like a gazillion texts, but she doesn't answer," said Brooke. "She's off Snapchat and Insta. I'm verging on hostile, so I thought I'd call and see what you know."

"Immie doesn't answer anyone," said Jule.

"Where are you?"

Jule saw no reason to lie. "San Francisco."

"You're here?"

"Wait, *you're* here?" La Jolla, where Brooke was supposed to be, was a good eight-hour drive away.

"I have high school friends who go to college in San Francisco, so I got a hotel and came up. But it turns out they all have jobs or exams up through today. I was supposed to meet Chip Lupton this morning, but he effing blew me off.

127

He didn't even text me till I was already waiting for him in, like, a hallway of dead snakes."

"Dead snakes?"

"Ugh," Brooke moaned. "I'm at the Academy of Sciences. Effing Lupton said he wanted to go see the herpetology exhibit. I want to get in his pants or I'd never have said yes. Is Immie in San Francisco with you?"

"No."

"When the eff is Hanukkah? Is she going home for that?"

"It's now. She wouldn't go home for it. She went to Mumbai, maybe. I don't know for sure."

"Okay. So come down, since you're in town."

"To the snakes?"

"Yeah. God, I'm bored. Are you far away?"

"I have—"

"Don't say you have stuff to do. We'll keep texting Immie and force her to get back to us. Does she have phone service in Mumbai? We can email her if she doesn't. Come find me in the herp exhibit," said Brooke. "You have to make an appointment. I'll text you the number."

Jule wanted to see *all the things*. She hadn't been to the Academy of Sciences yet. Plus she wanted to know what Brooke knew about Imogen's life after the Vineyard. So she jumped in a cab.

The Academy was a natural history museum full of dinosaur bones and taxidermy. "I have a two o'clock appointment," Jule told the man at the herp desk.

"ID, please."

Jule showed him the Vassar ID and he let her pass.

"We have more than three hundred thousand specimens from one hundred and sixty-six countries," he said. "Enjoy your day."

The collection was housed in a series of rooms. The vibe was half library, half storage facility. On the shelves stood glass bottles filled with preserved animals: snakes, lizards, toads, and many creatures Jule could not identify. They were all carefully labeled.

Jule knew Brooke was waiting for her, but she didn't text to say she'd arrived. Instead, she walked slowly along the aisles, keeping her feet silent.

She retained the names of most of the things she looked at. *Xenopus laevis*, African clawed frog. *Crotalus cerastes*, sidewinder. *Crotalus ruber*, red diamond rattlesnake. She logged the names of vipers, salamanders, rare frogs, tiny snakes native only to faraway islands.

The vipers were coiled upon themselves, suspended in dingy liquid. Jule touched her hand to their venomous mouths, feeling fear skim through her.

She turned a corner and found Brooke sitting on the floor in one aisle, staring at a robust yellow frog on a low shelf.

"Took you forever," Brooke said.

"I got into the snakes," said Jule. "They're so powerful."

"They're not powerful. They're dead," said Brooke. "They're, like, coiled up in bottles and nobody loves them. God, wouldn't it be depressing if after you died your relatives, like, preserved you in formaldehyde and kept you in a giant jar?"

"They have poison inside them," said Jule, still talking about the vipers. "Some of them can kill an animal thirty times their size. Don't you think that would be an amazing feeling, to have a weapon like that inside you?"

"They're so damn ugly," said Brooke. "It wouldn't be worth it. Whatever. I'm sick of herps. Let's get espresso."

The snack bar served tiny mugs of deeply bitter coffee and Italian gelato. Brooke told Jule to order vanilla and they poured the espresso over their dishes of ice cream.

"It has a name," said Brooke, "but I didn't pay attention when we went to Italy. We had it at this little restaurant on some square. My mother kept trying to tell me the history of the square, and my father was all, 'Let's practice your Italiano!' But my sister and I were bored. We were like that for the whole trip, our eyes rolling up, but then—and this happened nearly every time—the food would come and we would just be all, nom nom nom. Have you been to Italy? It's a level of pasta you don't even understand, I promise you. It shouldn't be legal." She lifted her bowl and drank the last of the espresso from it. "I'm coming home with you for dinner," she announced.

They hadn't talked about Imogen yet, so Jule said all right.

They bought sausage, pasta, and red sauce. Brooke had a bottle of wine in the trunk of her car. At the apartment, Jule shoved the stack of mail upside down in a drawer and hid her wallet while Brooke wandered around.

"Cool place." Brooke fingered the hedgehog pillows and the jars of pretty marbles and rhinestones. She took in the patterned tablecloth, red kitchen cabinets, decorative statues, and books that had belonged to the apartment's previous inhabitant. Then she opened cupboards and filled a pot with water for the pasta. "You need a Christmas tree," she said. "Wait, are you Jewish? No, you're not Jewish."

"I'm not anything."

"Everyone is something."

"No."

"Don't be weird, Jule. Like, I'm Pennsylvania Dutch on my mom's side and Irish Catholic and Cuban on my dad's side. That doesn't mean I'm a Christian, but it means I have to drive back home Christmas Eve and pretend to pay attention at midnight Mass. What are you?"

"I don't celebrate." Jule wished Brooke wouldn't push. She didn't have an answer. She had no mythology that resonated beyond the hero origin story.

"Well, that's effing sad," said Brooke, opening the bottle of wine. "Tell me where Immie's been."

"She and I came here," said Jule. "But just for a week. Then she told me she was going to Paris, said goodbye, and later texted that Paris was just a city like New York and she was going to Mumbai instead. Or else Cairo."

"I know she didn't go home because her mom emailed me again," said Brooke. "Oh, and I know she left Forrest. She texted that he was moping like a stripy sad cat and she was relieved to be rid of him, but she didn't give me the whole picture. Did she talk to you about the cleaner?"

This was the conversation Jule wanted to have, but she knew she had to tread carefully. "A little. What did she tell *you*?"

"She called me the day after I left the Vineyard and said everything was her fault and she was running off to Puerto Rico with you for some R and R," said Brooke.

"We didn't go to Puerto Rico," said Jule. "We came here."

"I effing hate how secretive she is," said Brooke. "I love her, but she's all about being, like, untethered and mysterious. It's so annoying."

Jule felt defensive of Imogen then. "She's trying to be true to herself instead of pleasing other people all the time," she said.

"Well, I wouldn't mind if she tried a little harder to please people, actually," said Brooke. "In fact, she could try a fuckload harder."

Brooke walked over to the television as if now she had said the definitive words on the subject of Imogen Sokoloff. She navigated for a little until she found an old Bette Davis movie that had just started. "Let's watch this," she said. She poured herself a second glass of wine and served the pasta.

They watched the film. It was black-and-white. Everyone wore wonderful clothes and behaved horribly to one another. After an hour, there was a knock on the door.

It was Maddie, the owner of the apartment. "I need to

turn the water in your bathroom sink on and then off again," she said. "The plumber is downstairs. He wants me to help him figure out why it's been acting up."

"Can you come back later?" said Jule.

"The guy is in my place right now," said Maddie. "I'll just be a minute. You'll barely know I'm here."

Jule glanced at Brooke. She had her feet on the coffee table. "Come in."

"Thanks, you're the best." Jule followed Maddie into the bathroom, where the owner messed with the faucets. "That should be enough," Maddie said, heading back out. "Now I'll go see if my sink is backed up. Hopefully I won't return."

"Thanks," said Jule.

"No, thank *you*, Imogen. Sorry to disturb your evening."

Damn.

Damn.

The door shut behind Maddie.

Brooke turned the TV off. She was holding her phone in her hand. "What did she say?"

"It's time for you to go home," said Jule. "You've had a lot to drink. I'm calling you a cab."

Jule kept up a steady stream of chatter until Brooke was in the car, but as soon as the cab pulled away, Immie's phone pinged in her pocket.

Brooke Lannon: Immie! where R you?

BL: Jule says Mumbai? Or Cairo.

BL: Zat true?

BL: Also, Vivian was a huge witch to me and I can't believe the thing about her and Isaac. I mean, I can believe it, but fuck.

BL: Chip Lupton felt my boob last night and then today he blew me off. So WHATEVER. Wish you were actually here, except it sucks so bad you'd hate it.

BL: Also, Jule told the landlady her name is Imogen. ????!!!!

Jule finally texted back.

IS: Hey. I'm here.

BL: Hi!!!!!

IS: Chip felt your boob?

BL: It takes boobs to make you text me back heh heh.

BL: Well, boobs are v. important.

Jule waited a minute and then texted:

IS: Relax about Jule. She is my oldest friend.

IS: I got her an apartment till she gets herself set up.

Signed the lease, so the owner thinks she's me. She's broke.

BL: Not convinced. She is off, somehow. For real, Jule let this lady CALL HER "IMOGEN."

IS: It's fine.

BL: IDK. Could mess up your credit rating and I know you care about that shit. Plus is creepy. Hello? Identity theft? Is actually a thing and not just an urban myth.

BL: Also, where are you? Mumbai?

Jule didn't answer. Nothing she could say mattered if Brooke was determined to make trouble.

11

Twelve weeks before Brooke came to dinner, Jule flew from Puerto Rico to San Francisco and checked into the Sir Francis Drake Hotel in Nob Hill. The place was all red velvet, chandeliers, and rococo flourishes. The ceilings were carved. Jule used Imogen's credit card and photo ID. The clerk questioned nothing and called her Ms. Sokoloff.

Jule had a suite on the top floor. The room had leather-studded chairs and a gold-tipped dresser. She began to feel better as soon as she saw it.

She took a long shower and washed the sweat of travel and the memories of Puerto Rico off her skin. She scrubbed hard with the washcloth and shampooed twice. She put on pajamas she'd never worn before and slept until the pain that ran up her neck finally disappeared.

Jule spent a week in that hotel. She felt like she was in an egg. The sparkling, hard shell of the hotel protected her when she needed it.

. . .

At the end of the week, she saw a listing, sent some emails, and went to see the San Francisco apartment. Maddie Chung toured her around. The place came furnished, but it didn't have the kind of plain furnishings you might expect from a rental apartment. It was filled with unusual pieces of sculpture and pretty collections in glass jars: buttons, marbles, and rhinestones displayed on shelves so they caught the light. The kitchen had red cabinets and wood floors. There were glass dishes and heavy cast-iron pans.

Handing over the key, Maddie explained that she had had a renter there for more than ten years, a single gentleman who had died without any relatives. "There was no one to tell when he died. No one to come and take his things," she said. "And he had such pretty taste, and had taken care of everything so well. I thought—I'll rent it furnished, like a vacation rental. Then people can appreciate it." She touched a jar of marbles. "No charity shop wants these."

"Why didn't he have anyone?" asked Jule.

"I don't know. He was only about my age when he died. Throat cancer. There were no next of kin I could discover. No money. Maybe he changed his name or fell out with his people. It happens." She shrugged. They were at the door now. "Do you have movers coming?" asked Maddie. "I ask because I like to be home if the door to the building is going to be propped open all day, but it shouldn't be a problem to arrange."

Jule shook her head. "I just have the suitcase."

Maddie looked at her kindly and then smiled. "Make yourself at home, Imogen. I hope you'll be happy here."

Hey, Mom & Dad,

I left Martha's Vineyard a little more than a week ago
and now I'm traveling. Not sure where I'll go! Maybe to
Mumbai or Paris or Cairo.

Island life was peaceful and kind of isolated from the rest
of the world. Everything moved at a slow pace. I'm really
sorry I haven't been in touch. I just need to figure out who I
am without school, or family, or anything else defining me.
Does that make sense?

I had this boyfriend on Martha's Vineyard. His name was
Forrest. But we've broken up now, and I want to see more
of the world.

Please don't worry about me. I will travel safely and take
good care of myself.

You've always been wonderful parents. I think about you
every day.

Much love,
Imogen

Once she set up her Wi-Fi in the San Francisco apartment,
Jule emailed this note from Imogen's account.

She also wrote to Forrest. She used Immie's favorite words, her slang, her sign-off, her "kind ofs" and
"maybes."

Hey Forrest.

This email is hard to write, but I have to tell you: I'm not coming back. The rent is paid up through the end of September, so as long as you're out before October 1, all's fine.

I don't want to see you again. I'm leaving. Well, ha. I'm already gone.

I deserve someone who doesn't look down on me. Admit it, you do. Because you're a man and I'm a woman. Because I'm smaller than you. Because I'm adopted, and you don't like to say it, but you value bloodlines. You think you're superior because I left college and you didn't. And you think writing a novel is more important than anything I like to do, or want to do with my life.

The truth is, Forrest, I'm the one with the power. I had the house. And the car. I paid the bills. I'm an adult, Forrest. You're nothing but an entitled, dependent little boy.

Anyway, I'm gone. I thought you should know why.
Imogen

Forrest wrote back. He was sad and sorry. Angry. Pleading. Jule didn't answer. Instead, she texted Brooke two kitty-cat vines with a short note.

IS: Broke up with Forrest. This stripy sad cat is maybe how he feels.
IS: The fluffy orange cat is how I feel. (So relieved.)

Brooke wrote back.

BL: Have you heard from Vivian?

BL: or anyone else from Vassar?

BL: Immie?

BL: Because I heard from Caitlin (Caitlin Moon not Caitlin
Clark) that

BL: Vivian is going out with Isaac now.

BL: But I don't believe any news I ever get from Caitlin
Moon.

BL: So maybe it isn't true.

BL: I just threw up a little in my mouth.

BL: I hope you're not upset.

BL: I am upset for you.

BL: But bye bye Forrest! Immie, you can do way better.

BL: OMG La Jolla is so boring la la la why don't you text
me back? text me back you witch

Later that same day, email came in from Vivian herself, reporting that she was in love with Isaac Tupperman and she hoped Imogen would understand because there is no controlling the human heart.

In the days that followed, Jule set about living mostly as she thought Immie would. One morning she knocked on Maddie Chung's door, carrying a latte from the café down the block. "I thought you might need a coffee."

Maddie's face lit up. Jule was invited in and met the wife, silver-haired and sleekly dressed, heading off to "run a corporation," said Maddie. Jule asked if she could see the bookstore, and the owner drove her over there in a Volvo.

Maddie's shop was small and untidy but comfortable. It sold a mix of used and new books. Jule bought two Victorian novels by writers she was not sure Immie had ever read: Gaskell and Hardy. Maddie recommended *Heart of Darkness* and *Dr. Jekyll and Mr. Hyde,* plus a book by some guy called Goffman titled *The Presentation of Self in Everyday Life.* Jule bought those as well.

Other days, Jule went to exhibits Maddie suggested. Thinking of Imogen, Jule slowed her pace and let her mind wander.

Immie wouldn't have paid close attention in any museum. She wouldn't have tried to learn art history and memorize dates.

No, Immie would have walked lazily through, allowing the space to dictate her mood. She'd have stopped to appreciate beauty, to exist without striving.

So much of Immie was in Jule now. That was consolation.

10

One week before she moved to San Francisco, Jule was drunk on the island of Culebra. She had never been drunk before.

Culebra is an archipelago off the coast of Puerto Rico. On the main island, wild horses walk the roads. Expensive hotels line the coasts, but the town center doesn't cater to tourists too much. The island is known for snorkeling, and a small American expat community exists there.

It was ten at night. The bar was a place Jule knew. It was open to the night air on one side. Dirty white fans whirred in the corners. The place was filled with Americans, some of them tourists but many of them expat regulars. The bartender didn't card Jule. Almost nobody asked for ID in Culebra.

Tonight, Jule had ordered a Kahlúa and cream. A man she'd met before bellied up a couple of seats down the bar. He was a bearded white guy, maybe fifty-five. He wore a Hawaiian shirt, and his forehead was sunburnt. He spoke with a West Coast accent—Portland, he'd told Jule earlier. She didn't know his name. With him was a woman of the same age. She had hair in messy gray curls. Her pink T-shirt showed cleavage, a little at odds with the print skirt and sandals she wore on her lower half. She started eating pretzel mix from a bowl on the bar.

Jule's drink arrived. She drained it and asked for another. The couple was arguing.

"That whore with a heart of gold: she was my main problem," said the woman in a Southern accent. Maybe Tennessee, maybe Alabama. Homey.

"It was just a movie," the man answered.

"The perfect girlfriend is a whore that does ya for free. Disgusting."

"I didn't know it was gonna be that," said the man. "I didn't even know it bothered you till we started walking over here. Manuel said it was a good movie. We put it on; not a big deal."

"It belittles half the population, Kenny."

"I didn't make you watch it. Besides, maybe it's open-minded about whoring." Kenny chuckled. "Like, we're not supposed to think less of her because of her job."

"You're supposed to say sex work," said the bartender, winking at them. "Not whoring."

Jule finished her drink and asked for a third.

"It was just stuff exploding and a guy in a red suit," Kenny said. "You've been hanging out with those book club friends too much. You always get sensitive after you hang out with them."

"Oh, up yours," the lady said, but she said it nicely. "You're so jealous of my book club friends."

Kenny noticed Jule looking at them. "Hey there," he said, lifting his beer.

Jule felt the three Kahlúas wash over her like a sticky wave. She smiled at the lady. "That's your wife," she said thickly.

"I'm his girlfriend," said the lady.

Jule nodded.

The evening began to tilt. Kenny and his lady, they were talking to her. Jule was laughing. They said she should eat some food.

She couldn't find her mouth. The French fries were too salty.

Kenny and his lady were still talking movies. The lady hated the guy in the red suit.

Who was that guy? Did he have a raccoon? He was friends with a tree. No, a unicorn. The guy made of rocks was always sad. He was stuck being rocks all the time, so nobody loved him. Then there was the one who didn't talk about who he was. He was old, but he had a good body and a metal skeleton. Wait, wait. There was a blue guy, too. And a naked woman. Two blue people. Suddenly Jule was on the floor of the bar.

She didn't know how she got there. Her hands were sore. There was something wrong with her hands. Her mouth felt strange and sweet. So much Kahlúa.

"You staying at Del Mar, the resort up the road?" Kenny's lady said to Jule.

Jule nodded.

"We should walk her back, Kenny," the lady said. She

was squatting on the floor by Jule. "That road's not lit. She could wander in front of a car."

Then they were outside. Kenny wasn't anywhere near them. The lady was holding Jule's arm. She walked Jule up the dark road to where the lights of the Del Mar shone.

"I need to tell you a story," Jule said loudly. She had to say stuff to Kenny's lady.

"Do you, now?" the lady said. "Watch your feet, there. It's dark."

"It's a story about a girl," said Jule. "No, a story about a boy. Long time ago. This boy, he pushed a girl he knew against a wall. Some other girl, not me."

"Um-hm."

Jule knew she wasn't telling it the way it needed to be told, but she was telling it. Now she wouldn't stop. "He had his ugly way with that girl in the alley behind the supermarket, in the night. Right? You know what I mean?"

"I think so."

"This girl knew him from around town and went back there with him when he asked her to because he had a pretty face. This stupid girl didn't know how to say no the right way. Not with her fists. Or maybe it didn't matter what she said because he didn't listen. Point is, this girl had no muscle. No skills. She had a plastic baggie full of milk and doughnuts."

"Are you from the South, honey?" said Kenny's lady. "I didn't notice before. I'm from Tennessee. Where you from?"

"She didn't tell any grown-ups what happened, but she told a couple friends in the ladies' room. That was how I found out about it."

"Uh-huh."

146

"This boy, this same boy, he was walking home from a movie one night. Two years later. I was sixteen and, you know, I'm in shape. Did you know that about me? I'm in shape. So one night I went to the movies and I saw him. I saw the boy as I was going home. I shouldn't have been on the street alone, most people woulda said. But I was. That boy shouldn't have been alone, either."

This whole idea suddenly seemed funny. Jule felt she needed to stop walking in order to laugh. She planted her feet and waited for the laugh to come. But it didn't.

"I had a blue slush in my hand," she went on, "the big kind you get at the movies. Strappy heels. It was summer. Do you like pretty shoes?"

"I have bunions," said the lady. "Come on, let's walk now."

Jule walked. "I took off my shoes. And I called that boy's name. I told him a fib about needing to call a cab, there on the corner in the dark. I said my phone was dead and could he help me? He thought I was harmless. I had a shoe in one hand and a drink in the other. My second shoe was on the ground. He came over. I tossed the slush in his face left-handed, swung at him with the heel. It hit him in the temple."

Jule waited for the lady to say something. But the lady was silent. She kept hold of Jule's arm.

"He lunged for my waist, but I brought up my knee and caught him in the jaw. Then I swung the shoe again. I brought it right down on the top of his head. Soft spot." It seemed important to explain exactly where the shoe had gone. "I hit him with the shoe, again and again."

Jule stopped walking and forced the lady to look her in the face. It was very dark. She could only see the kind wrinkles around the lady's eyes, but not the eyes themselves. "He lay with his mouth hanging open," Jule said. "Blood out his nose. He looked dead, ma'am. He didn't get up. I looked down the street. It was late. Not even a porch light was on. I couldn't tell if he was dead. I picked up the slush cup and my shoes and I walked home.

"I took everything I had been wearing and put it all in a plastic grocery bag. In the morning I pretended like I was going to school."

Jule dropped her hands to her sides. She suddenly felt tired and dizzy and empty.

"Was he dead?" Kenny's lady asked.

"He wasn't dead, ma'am," Jule said slowly. "I searched for his name online. I searched every day for it and it never came up, except in a local paper, next to a photograph. He won a poetry contest."

"For real?"

"He never reported what happened. That was the night I knew who I was," Jule told Kenny's lady. "I knew what I was capable of. Do you understand me, ma'am?"

"I'm glad he wasn't dead, honey. I think you're not used to drinking."

"I never drink."

"Listen. I had that thing happen to me, years back," said the lady. "Like that girl you talked about. I don't like to bring it up, but it's true. I worked through it and I'm all right now, you hear?"

"Yeah, okay."

"I thought you'd want to know that."

Jule looked at the lady. She was a beautiful lady, and Kenny was a lucky man. "Do you know Kenny's real name?" Jule asked. "What's Kenny's real name?"

"Let me take you to your room," the lady said. "I should make sure you get there all right."

"That was when I felt the hero inside me," said Jule.

After that she was in her room and the world went black.

Jule woke up the next morning with blisters. Each hand had four pus-filled lumps on the palms, just below the fingers.

She lay in bed and looked at them. She reached for her jade ring on the bedside table. It wouldn't slide on. Her fingers were too swollen.

She popped each blister and let the liquid soak into the soft white hotel sheet. The skin would callous over faster this way.

This isn't a movie about a girl who breaks up with her undermining boyfriend, she thought. This isn't a movie about a girl who breaks away from her controlling mother, either. It's not about some great white hetero hero who loves a woman he needs to save or teams up with a lesser-powered woman in a skintight suit.

I am the center of the story now, Jule said to herself. I don't have to weigh very little, wear very little, or have my teeth fixed.

I am the center.

As soon as she sat up, the gagging started. Jule rushed to the bathroom and pressed her blistered palms to the cool of the bathroom floor and heaved nothing into the toilet.

Nothing and more nothing. The gagging went on for what seemed like hours, her throat constricting and releasing. She pressed a washcloth to her face. It came back wet. She huddled around herself, shaking and heaving.

Finally, her breathing slowed.

Jule stood up. She made coffee and drank it. Then she opened Immie's backpack.

There was Immie's wallet. It had a million small pockets and a silver clasp. Inside were credit cards, receipts, a Martha's Vineyard library card, a Vassar ID, a Vassar dining hall meal card, a Starbucks card, a health insurance card, and the key card for Immie's hotel room. Six hundred and twelve dollars, in cash.

Jule opened Immie's package, delivered yesterday. Inside were clothes FedExed from an online retailer. Four dresses, two shirts, a pair of jeans, a silk sweater. Each item was so expensive Jule put her hand over her mouth involuntarily when she looked at the packing sheet.

Immie's room was next door. Jule had the key card now. The room was clean. In the bathroom, a grubby makeup bag sat on the counter. In it, Jule found Imogen's passport, plus a surprising number of tubes and compacts, all disorganized. On the towel rack hung an ugly beige bra. There was a razor with a few stray hairs in it.

Jule took Immie's passport and looked at the photograph next to her own face in the glass. The height difference was only an inch. The eye color was listed as green. Immie's hair was lighter. Jule's weight was significantly higher, but most of that was muscle and didn't show under certain clothes.

She pulled the Vassar IDs from Immie's wallet and looked at those. The meal card photo clearly showed Immie's long neck and her triple-pierced ear. The student ID was smaller and blurrier. It didn't show the ear. Jule could easily use that one.

She cut the meal card into tiny pieces with nail scissors and flushed the pieces down the toilet.

Then she plucked her eyebrows—thin, like Immie's. She

cut her bangs shorter with nail scissors. She found Immie's collection of vintage engraved rings: the amethyst fox, the silhouette, the wooden carving of the duck, a sapphire one with a bumblebee, a silver elephant, a silver leaping rabbit, and a green jade frog. They wouldn't fit on her swollen hands.

The next couple of days were spent going through Immie's computer files. Jule used both rooms. They were air-conditioned. Sometimes she opened a terrace door to let the thick heat pour in over her. She ate chocolate chip pancakes and drank mango juice from room service.

Immie's bank and investment accounts had a total of eight million dollars in them. Jule memorized numbers and passwords. Phone numbers and email addresses, too.

She learned Imogen's looping signature from the passport and the inside flaps of Immie's books. She copied other handwriting from a notepad Immie had, which was covered with doodles and shopping lists. After creating an electronic signature, she found the name of Immie's family lawyer. She told him she (Immie) would be traveling a lot in the next year, going around the world. She wanted to make a will. The money would be left to a friend who didn't have much, a friend who was an orphan and had lost her college scholarship: Julietta West Williams. She also left money to the North Shore Animal League and to the National Kidney Foundation.

It took a few days for the lawyer to take action, but he promised to arrange everything. No problem. Imogen Sokoloff was a legal adult.

She looked over Immie's writing style in emails and on Instagram: the way she signed off, the way she wrote paragraphs, the expressions she used. She closed all Immie's social media accounts. They were dormant anyhow. She untagged Immie from as many photographs as possible. She made sure all of Immie's credit cards auto-paid from Immie's bank accounts. She reset passwords using Immie's email.

She read the local Culebra paper for news, but there was nothing.

Jule bought hair color in a grocery store and streaked it on carefully with a toothbrush. She practiced smiling without showing her teeth. She had a bitter pain up one side of her neck that wouldn't leave.

Finally, the lawyer emailed a template will. Jule printed it out at the business office of the hotel. She put the papers in her suitcase and decided she'd waited long enough. She bought a ticket to San Francisco under Imogen's name. She checked out of the hotel for the two of them.

9

Two and a half weeks before she left for San Francisco, Jule sat next to Imogen in the back of a jeep taxi, bumping over the road from the Culebra airport. Immie had booked the resort.

"I came here with my friend Bitsy Cohan's family when we were twelve," Immie said, gesturing at the island around them. "Bitsy had her jaw wired shut after a bike accident. I remember she just drank virgin daiquiris all day. No food. One morning we got a boat over to this tiny island called Culebrita. It had black volcanic rock like nothing I ever saw before. And we snorkeled, but Bitsy's jaw caused snorkel problems, so she was very cranky."

"I had my jaw wired shut once," said Jule. It was true, but as soon as she said it, she wished she hadn't. It wasn't a funny story.

"What happened? Did you fall off a motorbike belonging to one of your Stanford boyfriends? Or did the evil coach of your track team put a hit out on you?"

"It was a locker room fight," Jule lied.

"Another one?" Immie looked ever so slightly disappointed.

"Well, we *were* naked," Jule said, to amuse her.

"Get out."

"After track practice, senior year of high school. Full-on naked battle, in the showers, three against one."

"Like a prison porno movie."

"Not as sexy. They broke my bloody jaw."

"Horses," said the driver, pointing, and sure enough there were. A group of three wild horses with sweetly shaggy coats stood in the middle of the road. The driver honked.

"Don't honk at them!" said Imogen.

"They're not scared," said the driver. "Look." He honked again and the horses moved slowly out of the way, only mildly annoyed.

"You like animals better than people," said Jule.

"People are assholes, as the story you just told completely proves." Imogen took a packet of tissues from her bag and used one to wipe her forehead. "When have you ever seen a horse be an asshole? Or a cow? They never are."

The driver spoke from the front of the car. "Snakes are assholes."

"They're not," said Immie. "Snakes are trying to get by, like everyone else."

"Not the biting ones," he said. "They're vicious."

"Snakes bite when they're scared," said Immie, leaning forward in the backseat. "They bite if they need to protect themselves."

"Or if they need to eat," said the driver. "They probably bite something once a day. I hate snakes."

"It's a lot nicer for a mouse to die from a rattlesnake bite than, say, to be caught by a cat. Cats play with their prey," said Immie. "They bat it around, let it escape, and then catch it again."

"Cats are assholes, then," the driver said.

Jule laughed.

They stopped in front of the hotel. Immie paid the driver in American dollars. "I stand by the snakes," said Imogen. "I like them. Thanks for the ride."

The driver pulled their suitcases out of the trunk and drove away.

"You wouldn't like a snake if you met one," said Jule.

"Yes, I would. I would love the snake and make a pet of it. I would twine it around my neck like jewelry."

"A venomous snake?"

"Sure. I'm here with you, aren't I?" Imogen slung her arm around Jule. "I'll feed you delicious mice and other kinds of snake snacks, and I'll let you rest on my shoulders. Every once in a while, when it's absolutely necessary, you can squeeze my enemies to death while naked. 'Kay?"

"Snakes are always naked," said Jule.

"You're a special snake. Most of the time you'll wear clothes."

Immie walked ahead into the hotel lobby, pulling both her suitcases behind her.

The hotel was glamorous in a touristy way, very turquoise. It had greenery and bright flowers everywhere. Jule and Imogen had rooms next to each other. There were two different pools and a beach that spread out in a long white arch with a dock at the far end. The menu was all fish and tropical fruits.

After unpacking, they met for dinner. Immie looked fresh and grateful to be eating such a gorgeous meal. She showed no trace of grief or guilt. Just existing.

Later they walked down the road to a place the Internet described as an expat bar. The counter was a wraparound, with the bartender in the center. They sat on wicker stools. Immie ordered Kahlúa and cream, while Jule got a Diet Coke with vanilla syrup. The people were talkative. Imogen took up with an old white guy in a Hawaiian shirt. He told them he'd lived on Culebra for twenty-two years.

"I had a little marijuana business," the guy said. "I used to grow it in my walk-in closet with lights and then sell it. It was Portland. You wouldn't think anyone there would care. But the cops busted me, and when I was out on bail I took a flight to Miami. From there I got a boat over to PR, then from there took the ferry here." He gestured to the bartender for another beer.

"You're on the lam?" asked Immie.

He snorted. "Think of it this way: I didn't believe that what I did should have been a criminal offense and so I didn't deserve the consequences that were coming my way. I relocated. I'm not running. Everyone here knows me. They don't know the name on my passport, is all."

"And what is that name?" asked Jule.

"I'm not telling you." He laughed. "Just like I don't tell them. Nobody bothers about stuff like that here."

"What do you do for a living?" Jule asked.

"There's a lot of Americans and rich Puerto Ricans who own vacation homes here. I take care of their houses for them. They pay in cash. Security, arranging for repairs, that kinda thing."

"What about your family?" Immie asked.

"Don't have much. I got a lady friend here. My brother knows where I am. He's come to visit me once or twice."

Imogen wrinkled her forehead. "Do you ever want to go back?"

The man shook his head. "I never think about it. You stay away long enough, there doesn't seem like much to go back for."

They spent the next three days sitting by the enormous curving pool, surrounded by umbrellas and turquoise lounge chairs. Jule was twined around Imogen's neck. They read. Imogen watched YouTube videos on cooking techniques. Jule worked out in the gym. Imogen got spa treatments. They swam and walked on the beach.

Imogen drank a lot. She had waiters bringing her margaritas poolside. But she didn't seem sad. The magic feeling of their initial escape from Martha's Vineyard threaded itself through the days. As far as Jule could tell, they were triumphant. This was the life Imogen described herself as wanting, free of ambition and expectations, with nobody to please and nobody to disappoint. The two of them just existed, and the days were slow and tasted of coconut.

Late on the fourth night, Jule and Immie sat with their feet in the hot tub, just as they had so many nights at Immie's house on the Vineyard. "Maybe I should go back to New York," said Imogen thoughtfully. "I should see my parents." They had eaten dinner a while ago. She had a margarita in a plastic cup with a lid and a straw.

"No, don't," said Jule. "Stay here with me."

"That guy in the bar the other night? He said the longer you don't go back, the less there is to go back to." Imogen stood, then, and pulled off her shirt and shorts. She wore a gunmetal one-piece with a gold hoop at the chest and a deep plunge. She sank her body slowly into the hot tub. "I don't want there to be nothing left. With my mom and dad. But I also hate being there. They just—they make me so sad. Last time I was home, did I tell you this? About winter break?"

"No."

"I left school and I was so glad to get away. I had failed political science. Brooke and Vivian were squabbling all the time. Isaac had dumped me. And when I got home, my dad was way more sick than I'd expected. My mom was in tears all the time. My stupid pregnancy scare and friendship drama and boyfriend problems and bad grades—it was all too trivial to even mention. My dad was shriveled into himself, breathing from his oxygen tank. The kitchen table was covered in pill bottles. One day he clutched my arm and whispered, 'Bring your old man a babka.'"

"What's a babka?"

"You never had babka? It's like a cinnamon roll times forty."

"Did you bring him one?"

"I went out and bought six babkas, and gave him one every day till winter break was over. It gave me something to do for him, when there wasn't anything, really, to do. . . . Then the morning I left, while my mom was driving me up to Vassar, I got hit with dread. I didn't want to see Vivian. Or Brooke. Or Isaac. College seemed pointless, like a finishing school where I was going to learn to be the kind of daughter my mother wanted me to be. Or the kind of girl Isaac wanted me to be. But not what *I* wanted to be, at all. As soon as she left, I called a taxi and went to the Vineyard."

"Why there?"

"An escape. We had been on vacation there when I was

little. After the first couple days I let my phone go dead. I didn't want to answer to anybody. I know that must sound selfish, but I had to do something radical. With my dad that sick, I hadn't talked to anyone about my problems. The only way I could figure myself out was to try what life was like *away*. Without all those other people wanting things from me, being disappointed in me. And then I just stayed. I had been living in the hotel for a month when I realized I wasn't going back. I emailed my parents that I was okay, and I rented the house."

"How did they react?"

"A thousand billion emails and texts. 'Please come home, just for a couple days. We'll pay for the plane.' 'Your father wants to know why you don't return his calls.' That kind of thing. My dad's dialysis prevented them from coming to the Vineyard, but they were literally harassing me." Immie sighed. "I blocked their texts. I stopped thinking about them. It felt like magic, just switching those thoughts off. Being able not to think about them saved me, somehow. I might be a terrible person, but it was so nice, Jule, not to feel guilty anymore."

"I don't think you're a terrible person," Jule said. "You wanted to change your life. You had to do something extreme to become the person you're becoming."

"Exactly." Immie touched Jule's knee with her wet hand. "Now, what about you?" It was Imogen's usual pattern, to talk in a long ramble until she had thoroughly sorted through an idea, then, tired, to ask a question.

"I'm not going back," said Jule. "Not ever."

"It's that bad back home?" Immie asked, searching Jule's face.

Jule thought for a bright second then that someone could love her, and that she could love herself and deserve it all. Immie would understand anything Jule said just now. Anything.

"We're the same," she ventured. "I don't want to be that person I was, growing up. I want to be the me who's here, now. With you." It was as true a statement as she knew how to make.

Immie leaned over and kissed her cheek. "Families are effed up the world over."

Jule's words rushed out of her. "We're each other's family now. I am yours and you can be mine."

She waited. Looked at Immie.

Imogen was supposed to say they were like sisters.

Imogen was supposed to say they were friends for life and that yes, they were family.

They had just talked so intimately, and Imogen was supposed to promise that she would never leave Jule like she'd just left Forrest, like she'd left her mother and her father.

Instead, Immie smiled mildly. Then she got out of the hot tub and walked over to the pool in that gunmetal bathing suit. She smiled at the cluster of teenage boys who were horsing around in the shallow end. American boys.

"Hey, guys. Does one of you want to get me a bag of potato chips or pretzels from the bar inside?" Immie said. "My feet are wet. I don't want to track water in there."

They were wetter than she was, but one of them jumped

out of the pool and toweled himself off. He was skinny and pimply but had good teeth and the kind of long, narrow body Immie liked. "At your service," he said, with a silly bow.

"You're a prince among men."

"See?" the boy called to his friends in the pool. "I'm a prince."

Why did Immie have to charm everyone? They were only a pack of boys, with little to offer. But Immie did this kind of thing whenever situations became intense. She turned and shined her light on new people, people who felt lucky she had noticed them. She had done it when she ditched her friends at Greenbriar for new friends who went to the Dalton School. She had done it when she'd left her sick father and her Dalton friends to go to Vassar, and when she'd left Vassar to live on Martha's Vineyard. She'd left Forrest and Martha's Vineyard for Jule, but Jule wasn't novel enough, apparently. Immie needed fresh admiration.

The boy brought out several bags of potato chips. Imogen sat on a lounge chair, eating and asking him questions.

Where were they from? "Maine."

How old were they? "Old enough! Ha ha."

No, really, how old? "Sixteen."

Imogen's laugh echoed out across the pool. "Babies!"

Jule stood and slid her shoes back on. There was something about those boys that made her skin crawl. She hated the way they competed to keep Imogen entertained, splashing and showing off their muscles in the pool. She didn't want to talk to a bunch of fawning high schoolers. Let Imogen feed her ego if she needed to.

The next morning, Jule wanted to rent a boat and go to Culebrita. That was the tiny island with the black volcanic rocks, a wildlife preserve with beaches. Immie had talked about it on their first day. You could go by water taxi, but then you had to wait for pickup. It was nicer to drive yourself, because then you could leave when you wanted to. The concierge gave Jule the phone number of a guy with a boat for rent.

Immie saw no need for them to take themselves when someone else could do it for them. She saw no need to go to Culebrita at all. She had seen it already. And there was clear, bright water right here. And a restaurant. And two heated pools. There were people to talk to.

But Jule couldn't stand a day at the pool with those high school boys, lumpish little show-offs. Jule wanted to go to Culebrita and see the famous black rocks and hike up to the lighthouse.

The boat guy said he'd meet them on the dock that extended from the far end of the beach. It was very informal. Jule and Immie walked down, and two young Puerto Rican men drove up in two small boats. Immie paid in cash. One guy showed Jule how to work the motor and how the oars fit on the edge of the boat, just in case you needed them. There was a number to call when they were done with the boat.

Immie was sulky. She said the life jackets were cracked and the boat needed a paint job. But she got in it anyway.

The ride across the bay took half an hour. The sun grew hot. The water was shockingly blue.

On Culebrita, Jule and Imogen jumped into the water to

push the boat onshore. Jule chose a path, and they started walking. Immie was silent.

"Which way?" Jule asked her at a fork in the trail.

"Whatever you want."

They went left. The hill was steep. After a fifteen-minute walk, Immie scraped her instep on a rock. She lifted her foot up and rested it against a tree to examine it.

"You okay?" Jule asked.

Immie was bleeding, but only slightly. "Yeah, fine."

"I wish we had a Band-Aid," said Jule. "I should have packed some."

"But you didn't, so it's fine."

"Sorry."

"It's not your fault," said Immie.

"I mean, I'm sorry it happened to you."

"Leave it," Imogen said, and continued walking up the hill. Cresting it, they arrived at the black rocks.

They were different than Jule expected. More beautiful. Almost frightening. They were dark and slippery. Water flowed in and around them, making pools that looked warm in the sun. Some of the rocks were covered with soft green algae.

There was no one else around.

Immie stripped down to her bathing suit and slid into the largest pool without a word. She was tan and wore a black bikini with a string around the neck.

Jule felt like a thick, masculine person suddenly. The muscles she worked so hard on seemed oafish, and the pale blue suit she'd worn all summer tacky.

"Is it warm?" she asked, about the shallow pool.

"Pretty warm," said Immie. She was bent over, splashing water up her arms and across the back of her neck. Jule was annoyed with Immie for sulking. After all, it wasn't her fault that Imogen had scraped her foot. All Jule was guilty of was saying she wanted to rent a boat and see Culebrita.

Immie was a spoiled child who pouted when she didn't get her way. It was one of her limitations. No one ever said no to Imogen Sokoloff.

"Shall we go up to the lighthouse?" Jule asked. It was the highest point on the island.

"We can."

Jule wanted Immie to show enthusiasm. But Immie wouldn't.

"Is your foot okay?"

"Probably."

"Do you *want* to walk up to the lighthouse?"

"I could."

"But do you want to?"

"What do you want me to say, Jule? 'Oh, it is my dream to see a lighthouse'? On the Vineyard I saw an effing lighthouse every single day of my life. You want me to say I am dying to hike up there with my bloody foot in this crazy heat to see a tiny building that looks like a million tiny buildings I've seen a million times before? Is that what you want?"

"No."

"What do you want, then?"

"I was just asking."

"I want to go back to the hotel."

"But we just got here."

Imogen climbed out of the water and pulled on her

clothes, shoving her feet into her sandals. "Can we please go back? I want to call Forrest. My phone doesn't work here."

Jule dried her legs off and put on her shoes. "Why do you want to call Forrest?"

"Because he's my boyfriend and I miss him," said Immie. "What did you think? That I broke up with him?"

"I didn't think anything."

"I didn't break up with him. I came to Culebra for a break, is all."

Jule shouldered the bag they were sharing. "You want to go back, let's go back."

Jule felt drained of all the joy she'd felt the past few days. Everything seemed hot and ordinary.

They had pulled the boat pretty far onshore, and when they returned to the beach they had to push it across the sand. Then they jumped in and dislodged the oars from the rack, using them to guide the boat into water deep enough that it began to float and they could start the motor.

Imogen didn't speak much.

Jule started the engine and pointed toward Culebra, which was visible in the distance.

Immie sat at the front end of the boat, her profile dramatic against the sea. Jule looked at her and felt a surge of affection. Immie was beautiful, and in her beauty you could see that she was kind. Good to animals. The type of friend who brings you coffee made just the way you like it, buys you flowers, gives you books, and bakes you muffins. No one knew how to have fun like Immie. She drew people to her; everyone loved her. She had a kind of power—money, enthusiasm, independence—that glowed around her. And here Jule was, out on the sea, this crazy turquoise sea, with this rare, unique human being.

Nothing of their quarrel mattered. It was fatigue, that was all. People argued in the best friendships. It was part of being real with one another.

Jule cut the engine. The sea was very quiet. There was not another boat anywhere on the horizon.

"Everything okay?" Imogen asked.

"I'm sorry I made us rent this stupid boat."

"It's okay. But listen, please. I'm going back to the Vineyard to be with Forrest tomorrow morning."

Jule felt dizzy. "How come?"

"I told you, I miss him. I feel bad about the way I left. I was upset about . . ." Immie paused, hesitant to put it into words. "About what happened with the cleaner. And about how Forrest handled it. But I shouldn't have run away. I run away too much."

"You shouldn't go back to the Vineyard because you feel obligated to Forrest, of all people," said Jule.

"I love Forrest."

"Then why are you lying to him all the time?" snapped Jule. "Why are you here with me? Why are you still thinking about Isaac Tupperman? That's not how you act when you're in love. You don't leave a person in the middle of the night and expect they'll be glad when you turn up again. You don't get to leave them like that."

"You're jealous of Forrest. I get that. But I'm not some doll you can play with and not share." Immie spoke harshly. "I used to think you liked me for myself—without my money, without anything. I thought we were alike and that you understood me. It was easy to tell you things. But more and more, I feel like you have this idea of me, *Imogen Sokoloff*"— she said her name as if it were in italics—"and it's not who I am. You have this idea of a person you like. But it's not me. You just want to wear my clothes and read my books and play pretend with my money. It's not a real friendship, Jule. It's not a real friendship when I pay for everything and you borrow everything and it's still not enough. You want all my secrets, and then you hold them over me. I feel sorry for you,

I do. I like you—but you've become, like, an imitation of me half the time. I'm sorry beyond sorry to have to say this, but you—"

"What?"

"You don't add up. You keep changing the details of the stories you tell, and it's like you don't even know it. I should never have asked you to come stay with us in the Vineyard house. It was good for a while, but now I feel used, and even lied to, somehow. I need to get away from you. That's the truth."

The sense of dizziness increased.

Immie couldn't be saying what she was saying.

Jule had been doing whatever Imogen wanted for weeks and weeks. She had left Immie alone when she wanted to be alone, had gone shopping when Immie wanted to go shopping. She had tolerated Brooke, tolerated Forrest. Jule had been a listener when required, a storyteller when required. She had adapted to the environment and learned all the codes of behavior for Immie's world. She had kept her mouth shut. She had read hundreds of pages of Dickens.

"I'm not my clothes," Imogen said. "I'm not my money. You want me to be this person—"

"I don't want you to be anything that's not yourself," interrupted Jule. "I don't."

"But you do," said Imogen. "You want me to pay attention to you when I don't feel like it. You want me to be beautiful and effortless, when some days I feel ugly and things come hard. You set me up on a throne and you want me to always make nice food and read great literature and be golden with everyone, but that isn't me, and it's exhausting.

I don't want to dress up and perform this idea you have of me."

"That isn't true."

"The weight of it is enormous, Jule. It smothers me. You're pushing me to *be something* to you, and I don't want to be it."

"You're my closest friend." It was the truth, and it came out of Jule's chest, loud and plaintive. Jule had always skimmed past people. They weren't hers; they never made a mark on her, and she would miss no one. Jule had told a hundred lies to make Immie love her. She deserved that love in exchange for them.

Immie shook her head. "After a couple weeks at my place this summer? Your closest friend? Not even possible. I should have asked you to leave after the first weekend."

Jule stood. Immie was sitting on the edge of the front of the boat.

"What did I do to make you hate me?" Jule asked her. "I don't understand what I did."

"You didn't do anything! I don't hate you."

"I want to know what I did wrong."

"Look. I only asked you to come with me because I wanted you to keep quiet," said Imogen. "I asked you here to shut you up. There, that's it."

They were silent. That sentence stood between them: *I asked you here to shut you up.*

Imogen went on: "I can't take this trip anymore. I can't take you borrowing my clothes and looking at me the way you do, like I'm never enough and you're threatening me and you want me to care so much for you. I don't."

Jule didn't think, couldn't think.

She picked up an oar from the bottom of the boat. She swung it, hard.

The paddle end hit Imogen in the skull. Sharp edge first.

Immie crumpled. The vessel rocked wildly. Jule stepped forward and Immie's face turned up at her. Immie looked surprised, and Jule felt a moment of triumph: the opponent had underestimated her.

She brought the oar down again on that angel face. The nose cracked, and the cheekbones. One of the eyes bulged and gushed. Jule hit a third time and the noise was terrific, loud and somehow final. Imogen's jaw and the entitlement and beauty and uncaring self-importance, all of it was smashed by the power of Jule's right arm. Jule was the fucking victor, and for a quick moment it felt glorious.

Immie slid off her perch into the water. The boat tipped as her weight fell off. Jule stumbled back, hitting her hip hard against the side.

Immie splashed twice, struggling. Gasping. Her eyes were filled with blood. It leaked out into the turquoise water. Her white shirt floated out around her.

The feeling of triumph waned and Jule jumped into the sea, grabbing Immie by the shoulder. She wanted a response.

Immie owed her a response.

They weren't done yet, damn it. Immie couldn't run away. "What do you have to say to me?" Jule cried, treading water and lifting Immie up as best she could. "What do you have to say to me now?" Blood ran down her arms from Immie's face. "Because I'm not your fucking pet, and I'm not your fucking friend anymore, either, you hear?" Jule shouted. "You look the fuck down on me, but I'm the strong one, I'm the fucking strong one here. Do you see, Immie? Do you see?"

Jule tried to turn Immie over, to keep her face in the air, to keep her breathing, and listening, but the wounds were enormous. Imogen's face was pulpy and leaking blood from the ear, from the nose, from the smashed side of her cheek. Her body jerked and shook. Her skin was slippery, so slippery. She threw her limbs around, hitting Jule in the face with the back of a flailing hand.

"What the fuck do you have to say now?" Jule said again, begging. "What is it that you want to tell me?"

Imogen Sokoloff's body jerked once more, and then grew still.

The blood pooled around them both.

Jule climbed back in the boat and time stopped.

An hour must have passed. Maybe two. Maybe only a couple of minutes.

No fight had ever gone like this. It had always been action, heroics, defense, competition. Sometimes revenge. This was different. There was a body in the sea. The edge of a small ear, triple-pierced. The buttons on the cuff of the shirt, a cool blue against the white linen.

Jule had loved Immie Sokoloff as well as she knew how to love anyone. She really had.

But Immie hadn't wanted it.

Poor Immie. Beautiful, special Immie.

Jule's stomach heaved. She gagged and gagged over the side of the boat. She clutched the edge, thinking she was being sick, her shoulders shaking. She heaved, but nothing came up, and nothing came up. It went on for a minute or two before she realized she was crying.

Her cheeks were slick with tears.

She had not meant to hurt Imogen.

No, she had.

No, she hadn't.

She wished she had not.

She wished it could be undone. She wished she were a different human in a different body with a different life. She wished Immie had loved her back, and she sobbed because it would never happen now.

She reached out and took Immie's wet, limp hand. She held it, leaning far over the edge of the boat.

There was a sound from an airplane overhead.

Jule dropped Immie's hand and swallowed her tears. Her instinct for self-preservation kicked in.

She was quite far out to sea. A twenty-minute boat ride from Culebra, and ten minutes from Culebrita. Jule touched her hand to the water. There was a current running toward the open ocean from the well-traveled channel between the two islands. She pulled Immie's hand toward her until she was close enough that she could loop a rope underneath the arms, making sure to keep it loose so it wouldn't leave a mark. The rope was rough, and tying it was awkward. Jule's palms were sore with it, the skin rubbing off. It took several tries before she got it into a knot that would hold.

She started the engine and motored slowly out in the direction of the open water, following the current. When the sea grew dark and deep, when they were well outside the traveled way between Culebra and Culebrita, Jule untied the rope and let Imogen go.

The body sank very, very slowly.

Jule rinsed the rope and scrubbed it with a brush she found in a small box of supplies. Her hands were raw and bleeding slightly, but otherwise she was unmarked. She coiled the rope neatly and put it back where it belonged in the boat. She scrubbed and rinsed the oar.

Then she motored back.

"Miss Sokoloff?" The clerk in the lobby waved at Jule.

Jule stopped and looked at him.

He thought she was Imogen. No one had mistaken her for Imogen until now.

They didn't look that much alike, but of course they were two young white women, short, with cropped hair and freckles. They had the same East Coast inflection to their speech. They might pass for each other.

"There's a package that came for you, Miss Sokoloff," said the clerk, smiling. "I have it right here."

Jule smiled back. "You're made of sugar," she told him. "Thank you."

8

Six days before Jule took that package, the cleaner didn't show up for work at Immie's house on Martha's Vineyard. His name was Scott. He was maybe twenty-four, older than Immie, Jule, Brooke, and even Forrest, but Imogen still called him the cleaner.

Scott had been recommended by the owners of the rental house to do yard work and housekeeping. The pool and hot tub needed maintenance. The house was airy and windowed, with double-height ceilings in the living and dining rooms. Six skylights, five bedrooms. Decks in front and back. Rosebushes and other plantings. It was a lot to keep clean.

Scott had a wide, open face and a flat nose. He was white, with pink cheeks, a square face, and unruly dark hair. He had narrow hips and serious muscles in his arms. He usually wore a baseball cap and no shirt.

When Jule first met Scott, she couldn't quite tell what he was doing there. He was simply in the kitchen, cleaning the floor with a mop and a bucket. He seemed no different from Forrest and Immie's various temporary island friends, but here he was, naked to the waist, doing housework. "Hi, I'm Jule," she said, standing in the doorway.

"Scott," he said, still mopping.

"You coming to the beach?" she had asked.

"Ha, no. I'm good here. I'm Imogen's cleaner." His accent was general American.

"Oh, I see." Jule wondered if Imogen talked to the cleaner like a regular person, or if Scott was supposed to be invisible. She didn't know what the codes of behavior were yet. "I'm Immie's friend from high school."

He didn't say anything else.

Jule watched him for a bit. "You want a drink?" she asked. "There's Coke and Diet Coke."

"I should keep working. Imogen doesn't like me to sit around."

"She's that tight?"

"She knows what she wants. I gotta respect that," he said. "And she pays me."

"But do you want a Coke?"

Scott got on his knees and sprayed cleaning fluid in the area underneath the dishwasher, where dirt collected. Then he scrubbed at it with a rough sponge. The muscles of his back shone with sweat. "She doesn't pay me to take stuff out of her fridge," he finally answered.

In later days, it became clear that Scott was not precisely supposed to be invisible, because he was in fact so decorative that nobody could possibly ignore his presence, but no one talked to him beyond a hello. Immie just said "hey" when she saw him, though her eyes tracked his body. Scott scrubbed the toilets and took out the trash and straightened up messes people left in the living room. Jule never offered him a Coke again.

The day Scott didn't show up was a Friday. Friday mornings he usually cleaned the kitchen and bathrooms, then watered the lawn. He was out of the house by eleven a.m., so no one thought too much of his absence.

The next day, however, he didn't show up, either. On Saturdays he cleaned the pool and did garden maintenance. Immie always left him cash for the previous week's work on the kitchen counter. The cash was there as usual, but Scott never came.

Jule walked downstairs, dressed to work out. Brooke was sitting on the kitchen counter with a bowl of grapes. Forrest and Immie were eating granola with heavy cream and raspberries at the dining table. The sink was full of dishes. "Where's the cleaner?" Brooke called into the dining room as Jule poured herself a glass of water.

"He's annoyed with me," answered Immie.

"I'm annoyed with *him*," said Forrest.

"I'm annoyed, too," called Brooke. "I want him to wash my grapes, strip down, and lick my whole body from head to toe. And yet he is still not doing that. He's not even here. I don't know what went wrong."

"Very funny," said Forrest.

"He's everything I want in a guy," said Brooke. "He's built, he keeps his mouth shut, and unlike you"—she popped a grape in her mouth—"he does dishes."

"I do dishes," said Forrest.

Immie laughed. "You do like a single dish that you ate out of."

Forrest blinked and went back to the previous topic. "Did you call him yet?"

"No. He wants a raise and I won't give it to him," Immie said smoothly, glancing up at Jule and meeting her eyes. "He's fine, but he's been late lots of times. I hate waking up to a messy kitchen."

"Did you fire him?" asked Forrest.

"No."

"After you talked about the raise, did he say he'd keep working here?"

"I think so. I'm not sure." Immie stood up to clear her mug and bowl.

"How can you not be sure?"

"I thought so. But I guess he's not," Immie said from the kitchen.

"I'm calling him," said Forrest.

"No, don't." She came back into the dining room.

"Why not?" Forrest picked up Immie's phone. "We need a cleaner, and he already knows the job. Maybe there was a misunderstanding."

"I said, don't call him," snapped Immie. "That's my phone you're holding, and it is not your house."

Forrest put the phone down. He blinked again. "I'm being helpful," he said.

"No, you're not."

"Yes, I am."

"You leave everything here to me," Immie said. "I take care of the kitchen and the food and the cleaner and the shopping and the Wi-Fi. Now you're annoyed when I'm not handling something the way you want it?"

"Imogen."

"I'm not your effing housewife, Forrest," she said. "That's the opposite of what I am."

Forrest went to his laptop. "What's Scott's last name?" he asked. "I think we should search his name and see if anyone's complained about him, what his deal is. He must be listed on Yelp or something."

"Cartwright," said Immie, apparently willing to stop the argument. "But you're not going to find him. He's a Vineyard guy who does handyman stuff for cash. There won't be a website."

"Well, I can find out— Oh God."

"What?"

"Scott Cartwright of Oak Bluffs?"

"Yes."

"He's dead."

Immie rushed over. Brooke was off the counter, and Jule came back from the hall, where she'd been stretching. They clustered around the computer.

It was an article on the *Martha's Vineyard Times* website, reporting the suicide of one Scott Cartwright. He had hanged himself with rope from a beam high up in a neighbor's barn. He had kicked out a twenty-foot ladder.

"It's my fault," said Imogen.

"No, it's not," said Forrest, still looking at the screen. "He wanted a raise and he was consistently late. You wouldn't give him more money. That has nothing to do with him killing himself."

"He must have been depressed," said Brooke.

"It says here he didn't leave a note," said Forrest. "But they're sure it was a suicide."

"I don't think it was," Immie said.

"Come on," said Forrest. "Nobody forced him to climb up a twenty-foot ladder in a barn and hang himself."

"Yeah," said Immie. "I think maybe they did."

"You're overreacting," said Forrest. "Scott was a nice guy, and it's sad that he died, but nobody *killed* him. Act rational."

"Don't tell me to act rational," Immie said, her voice steely.

"Nobody's going to kill the cleaner and make it look like suicide." Forrest stood up from the computer. He twisted his long hair into a ponytail with an elastic he'd had on his wrist.

"Don't talk to me like I'm a child."

"Imogen, you're upset about Scott, which is understandable, but—"

"This is not about Scott!" cried Immie. "It's about you telling me to act rational. You think you're superior because you have a college degree. And because you're a man. And because you're a Martin of the Martins of Greenwich and—"

"Immie—"

"Let me finish," barked Imogen. "You live in *my* home. You eat *my* food and drive *my* car and have your messes cleaned up by that poor boy *I* used to pay. Some part of you hates me for that, Forrest. You hate me because I can afford this life and I make my own decisions—so you patronize me and dismiss my ideas."

"Please, can we have this conversation in private?" asked Forrest.

"Just go. Leave me alone for a while," said Immie. She sounded tired.

Forrest grunted and went upstairs. Brooke followed.

Immie's face crumpled into tears as soon as they were gone. She walked over to Jule and hugged her, smelling like coffee and jasmine. They stood like that for a long time.

Immie and Forrest drove off in the car twenty minutes later, saying they needed to talk. Brooke stayed in her room.

Jule worked out and then killed the morning on her own. For lunch she ate two pieces of toast with chocolate-hazelnut spread and drank protein powder mixed with orange juice. She was washing up when Brooke clomped downstairs and dragged her duffel bag into the living room.

"I'm off," said Brooke.

"Right now?"

"I don't need the drama. I'm going home to La Jolla. My parents will be like, *Brooke, you should get an internship! Volunteer! Go back to school!* So it'll be extremely annoying, but you know, I'm kind of homesick, actually." Brooke turned abruptly and walked into the kitchen. She yanked open the pantry door and took two boxes of cookies and a bag of tortilla chips, shoving them into her shoulder bag. "The food on the ferry is trash," she said. "Bye."

In the evening, Imogen returned. She came out to see Jule on the deck.

"Where's Forrest?" Jule asked.

"He went up to his study." Immie sat down and took off her sandals. "There's a memorial service for Scott next weekend."

"Brooke left."

"I know. She texted me."

"She took all the cookies with her."

"Brooke."

"She said you wouldn't care."

"I wasn't saving them." Imogen stood and walked over to the switch that flipped the pool lights on. The water lit up. "I think we should go away. Without Forrest."

Yes.

Would it really be this easy? To have Immie for herself?

"I think we should leave in the morning," Imogen continued.

"Okay." Jule made herself sound nonchalant.

"I'll get us a flight. You understand. I need to get out of here, have some girl time."

"I don't need to be here," said Jule, glowing. "I don't need to be anywhere."

"I have an idea," said Imogen conspiratorially. She stretched back out on the lounge. "This island called Culebra. It's off Puerto Rico." Immie reached out and touched Jule's arm. "And don't worry about the money. Tickets, hotel, spa treatments—on me."

"I'm all yours," said Jule.

7

Two days before he died, Scott was cleaning the pool when Jule came back from her morning run. He had his shirt off. His jeans were low on his hips. He was trailing a leaf skimmer along the edges of the water.

He said good morning brightly as Jule passed him. Immie and Forrest weren't up yet. Brooke's rental car wasn't in the driveway. Jule grabbed a pile of clothes she'd laid out earlier and hung them up on the hook next to the outdoor shower. Then she went in.

She washed, shaved her legs, and thought about Scott. He was very, very pretty. She wondered about his lat workouts and his all-cash payments. How had he become a guy who was willing to bleach other people's toilets and mow their yards? He looked and sounded like the great white hetero action hero you saw in movie after movie. He could probably have most things he wanted in this world without too much effort. Nothing was pushing him down, but here he was. Cleaning.

Maybe he liked it that way. But maybe he didn't.

When she turned off the water, Scott and Imogen were talking on the deck.

"You have to help me," he said, his voice low.

"No, I don't, actually."

"Please."

"I can't get involved."

"You don't have to be involved, Imogen. I came to you for help because I trust you."

Immie sighed. "You came to me because I have a bank account."

"That's not it. We have a connection."

"Hello?"

"All those afternoons at my place. I didn't ask for anything. You came there because you wanted to."

"I haven't been to your place for a week," said Imogen to Scott.

"I miss you."

"I'm not paying your debt." Immie's voice was firm.

"I just need a loan. To get by. Till these guys get off me."

"It's a bad idea," said Imogen. "You should go to the bank. Or borrow against a credit card."

"I don't have a credit card. These guys are—they're not messing around. They left notes inside my car. They—"

"You shouldn't have been gambling," snapped Immie. "I thought you were smarter than that."

"Can't you front me enough to get this debt paid off? Then you won't have to see me again. I'll pay you back and disappear, I promise."

"A minute ago you were all about what a great connection we have. Now you're promising to disappear?"

"I have nothing," pleaded Scott. "There's five bucks in my wallet right now."

"Where's your family?"

"My dad split a long time ago. My mom got cancer when I was seventeen," said Scott. *"I don't have anybody."*

Immie was silent for a moment. "I'm sorry. I didn't know that."

"Please, Immie. Cupcake."

"Don't start with that. Forrest is upstairs."

"If you'll just help me, I can leave quietly."

"Is that a threat?"

"I'm asking for help from a friend to pay a debt, that's all. Ten thousand dollars is nothing to someone like you."

"Why do you owe the money? What did you bet on?"

Scott muttered his answer. "Dogfight."

"No." Immie sounded shocked.

"I had a good dog."

"Dogfighting is a blood sport. That's a felony."

"There was this rescue dog I knew about; she was a real scrapper. And I know a guy who sets up fights sometimes. He has a couple pit bulls. It wasn't, like, an organized thing."

"It was organized if this guy sets up fights. There are laws against that. It's cruel."

"This dog liked to fight."

"Don't say that," said Imogen. "Just don't. If someone adopted her and was kind with her, she would have—"

"You didn't meet this dog," said Scott, petulant. "Anyway,

189

we had the fight, and she lost, all right? I stopped it before she got hurt too bad, because you can if you're the owner of a dog, because she was— The fight wasn't what I thought it would be."

Jule held still, protected by the wall of the outdoor shower. She didn't dare move.

"That meant I lost money for all these guys who bet on her," Scott went on. "They said I should have let her play it to the death. I said the rules say an owner can stop the fight. They said yeah, but no one does that because you shaft all the people who bet on your dog." He was crying now. "And they want their bet money back. The guy who organized the fight wants his investment back, too. He says people complained, that I ruined his business by fighting a dog when I was . . . I'm scared, Imogen. I don't know how to fix this without your help."

"Let me explain the situation to you," Imogen said slowly. "You are my yard boy, my pool boy, my cleaner. You work here. You have done a decent job, and you've been a good guy to hang around with now and again. That does not put me under any obligation to help you when you have done an illegal and immoral thing to a poor, defenseless dog."

Jule began to sweat.

The way Imogen said *yard boy, pool boy, cleaner.* It was so cold. Jule hadn't seen Immie face to face with anyone she disdained until now.

"You won't help me, then?" Scott asked.

"We hardly know each other."

"Come on, you've come over to my house every day, some weeks."

"I never knew you liked to watch dogs tear each other to shreds until they die. I never knew you were a gambler. I never knew you were anything like so stupid and cruel as you are, because you are nothing more to me than the guy who cleans my house. I think you should go now," Imogen told Scott. "I can find someone else to scrub the floors."

Immie had been lying to Forrest. And to Jule. Immie had purposefully made up stories about where she went in the afternoons. She'd lied about why she'd come home with wet hair, about why she was tired, about where she'd bought her groceries. She'd lied about playing tennis with Brooke.

Brooke. Brooke must have known about Scott. She and Imogen had often come home together with rackets and water bottles, talking about their tennis games, when they had probably never played tennis at all.

Scott left without another word. A minute later, Immie banged on the shower door. "I can see your feet, Jule."

Jule gasped.

"Why do you listen to other people's conversations like that?" Immie barked.

Jule pulled the towel tighter around herself and opened the shower door. "I was drying off. You came outside. I didn't know what to do."

"You're always lurking around. Spying. No one likes it."

"I got it. Now can I please put my clothes on?"

Imogen walked away.

Jule wanted to follow and slap Immie's false, beautiful face.

She wanted to feel righteous and strong instead of embarrassed and betrayed.

But she'd have to burn off that anger another way.

She grabbed her swimsuit and goggles from a hook in the shower. In the pool, she swam a mile, freestyle.

A second mile. She swam until her arms were shaking.

Finally, she threw herself onto a towel on the wooden deck. She turned her face to the sun and felt nothing besides tired.

Imogen came out a little while later. She was carrying a bowl of warm chocolate chip muffins. "I baked these," she said. "To say sorry."

"Nothing to be sorry for," said Jule, not moving.

"Everything I said was mean. And I've been lying to you."

"Like I care."

"You do care."

Jule didn't answer.

"I know you care, bun. We shouldn't have lies between us. You understand me so much better than Forrest does. Or Brooke."

"Possibly true." Jule couldn't help herself. She smiled.

"You have a right to be mad. I was wrong. I know it."

"Possibly true as well."

"I think the whole thing was a means for me to push Forrest away. I do that when I get tired of guys. Cheat on them. I'm sorry I didn't tell you. I'm really not proud of myself."

Imogen set the muffins down by Jule's shoulder. She lay on the deck. Their bodies were parallel.

"I want to be at home somewhere, and I want to run away," Immie went on. "I want to be connected to people, and I want to push them away. I want to be in love, and I pick guys I'm not sure I even like all the way. Or I love them and I ruin it and maybe I ruin it on purpose. I don't even know which it is, and how messed up is that?"

"It's medium messed-up," said Jule, chuckling. "But not drastic. On a scale of one to ten, it's like a seven, I think."

They lay there in silence for another minute.

"But level seven messed-up is probably normal," Jule added.

"Can I pretty please bribe you with muffins to forgive me?" Immie asked.

Jule took a muffin and bit into it. "Scott is gorgeous," she said, swallowing. "Guy like that, what are you going to do: leave him alone and watch him clean the pool? I think you might have been legally obligated to jump him."

Imogen moaned. "Why did he have to be so sexy?" She grabbed Jule's hand. "I was such a witch. Forgive me?"

"Always."

"You are made of sugar, my bun. Come to the store with me now!" She said it like the store was going to be wonderfully fun.

"I'm tired. Make Brooke go with you."

"I don't want Brooke."

Jule stood up.

"Don't tell Forrest we're leaving," Immie said.

"I won't."

"Of course you won't." Imogen smiled up at Jule. "I know I can count on you. You won't tell him anything at all, will you."

6

📅 **END OF JUNE, 2016**

📍 **MARTHA'S VINEYARD, MASSACHUSETTS**

Ten weeks before Immie made the muffins, Jule found herself on Moshup Beach without a towel or a swimsuit. The sun was bright and the day hot. After the long trek down from the parking lot, she walked along the edge of the water. Huge clay cliffs loomed over her in colors of chocolate, pearl, and rust. The clay was cracked and slightly soft to the touch.

Jule took her shoes off and stood still with her toes in the sea. Some fifty yards away, Imogen and her friend set up for the afternoon. They had no beach chairs, but the guy unpacked a bag that held a cotton beach blanket, towels, magazines, and a small cooler.

They threw their clothes in the sand, put on sunblock, and drank from cans they took from the cooler. Imogen lay on the blanket to read. The guy collected rocks and piled them, one on top of another, to build a delicate sculpture in the sand.

Jule walked toward them. A few yards off she called: "Immie, is that you?"

Imogen didn't turn around, but her boyfriend poked her in the shoulder. "She's calling your name."

"Imogen Sokoloff, right?" Jule said, coming to stand over them. "It's me, Jule West Williams. Do you remember?"

Imogen squinted and sat up. Fumbled for her sunglasses in the mesh bag she carried and put them on.

"We were at school together," Jule went on. "At Greenbriar."

Immie was special to look at, Jule thought. A long neck, high cheekbones. Sun-kissed. She was skinny on top, though, and weak. "Were we really?" she asked.

"Only for part of freshman year. Then I transferred out," said Jule. "I remember you, though."

"Sorry, what's your name again?"

"Jule West Williams," said Jule again. When Imogen furrowed her brow, she added: "I was a year behind you."

Immie smiled. "Well, good to re-meet you, Jule. This is my boyfriend, Forrest."

Jule stood there awkwardly. Forrest was adjusting his lank hair back into its bun. A copy of the *New Yorker* sat next to him. "You want a drink?" he asked, surprisingly friendly.

"Thanks." Jule kneeled on the edge of the blanket and accepted a can of Diet Coke.

"You look like you're going somewhere," said Imogen. "With the bag, carrying your shoes."

"Oh, I—"

"Don't you have beach things?"

Jule thought of the most appealing thing she could say, and it turned out to be the truth. "I came on impulse," she said. "I do that sometimes. I hadn't planned on the beach today."

"I have an extra bathing suit in my bag," said Imogen, suddenly warm. "You want to go for a swim with us? I'm so effing hot, I have to get in the water now or I'll get heat exhaustion and Forrest will have to carry me back up that long-ass path." She ran her eyes over Forrest's narrow body. "I don't know if he's up to it. So you want to swim?"

Jule raised her eyebrows. "I could take you up on that."

Imogen pulled a bikini out of her bag and handed it to Jule. It was white and very minimal. "Wiggle it on under your skirt and we'll meet you in the water."

She and Forrest ran laughing into the sea.

Jule put on Imogen's clothes for the first time.

In Immie's suit, she dove under the waves and came up feeling miraculously happy. The day was sparkling, and it seemed impossible to be anything other than grateful for the chance to stand in the ocean, looking out at the horizon while the salt water smacked them around. Forrest and Immie didn't talk much but rode the waves, screaming and laughing. When they tired out, they stood on tiptoe beyond where the waves broke, jumping gently and letting the water carry them up and down. "Here comes a big one." "No, the one after is even bigger. There, see?" "Oh, damn, I almost died, but that was excellent."

When all three of them were blue in the fingers and shivering, they returned to Imogen's blanket, and Jule found herself in the center of it. Forrest lay on one side, wrapped in a nautical-themed towel, and Imogen lay on the other, face up to the sun and still covered in water droplets.

"Where did you go after Greenbriar?" Imogen asked.

"After they kicked me out," said Jule, "my aunt and I left New York."

"They did *not* kick you out," Imogen said gleefully. Forrest put down his magazine.

"Oh yes, they did." Both of them were interested now. "Prostitution," Jule said.

Imogen's face went dark.

"Kidding. That was a joke."

Imogen began laughing low and slowly, covering her mouth with her hand.

"Tina whatshername used to give me wedgies and say threatening shit to me in the locker room," said Jule. "Finally I banged her head against a brick wall. She ended up needing stiches."

"Was she that one with the curly hair? The tall one?" asked Imogen.

"No. The shorter one who followed that one around."

"I can't picture her."

"Better off that way."

"And you banged her head against the wall?"

Jule nodded. "I'm a scrapper. You could call it a talent."

"Scrapper?" Forrest asked.

"A fighter," said Jule. "Not for fun, but—you know. Self-defense. Battling evil. Protecting Gotham City."

"I can't believe I never heard about you sending a girl to the hospital," said Imogen.

"They kept it quiet. Tina didn't want to talk about it because of what she did to me *before* I made her stop, you know? And it made Greenbriar look bad. Girls fighting. It was right before winter concert," said Jule. "When all the parents come. They let me sing in it before they kicked me out. Remember? That Caraway girl had the solo."

"Oh, yeah. Peyton Caraway."

"We sang a Gershwin song."

"And 'Rudolph,'" said Imogen. "We were way too old to sing 'Rudolph.' It was ridiculous."

"You wore a blue velvet dress with darts down the front."

Imogen put her hands over her eyes. "I can't believe you remember that dress! My mother always made me wear stuff like that at the holidays, and we don't even celebrate Christmas. Like she was dressing up an American Girl doll."

Forrest poked Jule's shoulder. "You must be starting college in the fall."

"I finished high school early, actually. So I've been a year already."

"Where?"

"Stanford."

"Do you know Ellie Thornberry?" Imogen asked. "She goes there."

"I don't think so."

"Walker D'Angelo?" Forrest said. "He's in graduate art history."

"Forrest is done with college," said Imogen. "But for me it was like the halls of effing hell, so I'm not going anymore."

"You didn't really try," said Forrest.

"You sound like my dad."

"Oh, pout pout."

Immie put on her sunglasses. "Forrest's writing a novel."

"What kind of novel?" asked Jule.

"A little Samuel Beckett meets Hunter S. Thompson," said Forrest. "And I'm a big fan of Pynchon, so he's an influence."

"Good luck with that," said Jule.

"Ooh, you *are* a scrapper," said Forrest. "I kind of like her, you know, Imogen?"

"He likes ornery women," said Imogen. "It's one of his few endearing qualities."

"Do *we* like *him*?" Jule asked her.

"We tolerate him for his good looks," said Immie.

They declared themselves hungry and walked to the Aquinnah shops. The area had a cluster of snack stands. Forrest ordered three paper packets of french fries for them to share.

Immie smiled big at the guy behind the counter and said, "You're going to laugh at me, but I need like four slices of lemon for the Snapple. I'm crazy for lemon. Can you do that for me?"

He said, "Lemon?"

"Four slices," said Immie. She put her arms and elbows on the takeout counter and leaned forward, turning her face up to him.

"Of course," he said.

"You're laughing at my lemon," she told him.

"I'm not laughing."

"You're laughing on the inside."

"No." He had sliced the lemon by now and pushed it across the counter to her in a red-and-white paper cup.

"Thank you, then, for taking my lemon so seriously," Imogen said. She picked up one of the pieces and stuck it in her mouth, biting to squeeze out some of the juice. She said through her lemon-rind mouth: "It is very important for lemons to get respect. It makes them feel valued."

They sat at a picnic table with a view of the parking lot on one side and the sea on the other. People were flying kites on the other side of the parking lot. It was very windy. The picnic table was weathered gray and bumpy. Imogen ate one or two fries, and then took a banana out of her bag and ate it with a spoon.

"You're here alone?" asked Immie. "On the Vineyard?"

Forrest had opened his copy of the *New Yorker.* His body was turned slightly away from them.

Jule nodded. "Yes. I left Stanford." She told the story about the pervy coach and the loss of the scholarship. "I don't want to go home. I don't get along with my aunt."

Immie leaned forward. "Is that who you live with?"

"No, I'm not dealing with family anymore."

Forrest chuckled. "Neither is Imogen."

"Yes, I am," said Imogen.

"No, she's not," he said.

Jule looked Imogen in the eye. "We have that in common, then."

"Yes, I suppose we do." Immie tossed her banana peel in the trash. "Listen, come with us to the house. We can swim in the pool and you can stay for dinner. Some temporary people are coming over, new friends who are just on the island for a couple weeks. We're going to grill steaks. It's just in Menemsha. You won't believe the house. It's gargantuan."

The answer was yes, but Jule hesitated.

Imogen sat down close to Jule and lined their feet up together. "Come on. It'll be fun," she coaxed. "I haven't had any girl talk in ages."

The Menemsha house had ceilings so high and windows so wide that everyday activities seemed to have extra room and light. Drinks seemed fizzier and colder than any drinks ever had before.

Jule, Forrest, and Immie swam in the pool and then used the outdoor shower. The temporary people came for dinner, but Jule could already tell she wasn't one of them, from the way Imogen called her over to the grill to look at the steaks, and from the way she sat on the deck, curled up at Jule's feet. Imogen told her she should stay overnight in one of the guest rooms, just as the other friends were piling into their car. They offered to drive Jule back to her hotel, down the now-dark island roads.

She declined.

Immie showed Jule to a room on the second floor. It had a huge bed and flowing white curtains—and, oddly, a small antique rocking horse and a collection of old weather vanes arranged on a large wooden desk. Jule slept the deep sleep that comes of long days in the sun.

The next morning, Forrest sulkily drove her to the hotel to collect her things. When Jule walked in again with her suitcase, she saw that Immie had put four vases of flowers in the room. Four. She also left books on the bedside table: *Vanity Fair* by Thackeray and *Great Expectations* by Dickens, plus *The Insider's Guide to Martha's Vineyard*.

Thus began a series of days that blurred one into the

other. Immie's people, temporary and literary friends of the week, acquired on the beach or at the flea market, cycled through the house. They swam in the pool and helped with cookouts and laughed hysterically, clutching their chests. They were uniformly young: good-looking, effete boys and equally good-looking, loud girls. Most of them were funny and nonathletic, chatty and rather alcoholic, college kids or art students. Beyond that, they were of many backgrounds and sexual orientations. Imogen was a New York City child: open-minded in a way Jule had seen only on television, apparently utterly confident in her own desirability as a friend and hostess.

Jule took a day or two to adjust but soon found herself comfortable. She charmed the temporary people with stories of Greenbriar, Stanford, and, to a lesser extent, Chicago. She argued with them cheerfully when they wanted to argue. She flirted with them and forgot their names and let them know that she'd forgotten their names, because the forgetting made them admire her and want her to remember. At first, she texted Patti Sokoloff pictures and wrote chatty, hopeful emails, but it wasn't long before Jule ignored Patti just as Imogen did.

Immie made her feel wanted. The novel joy of it filled Jule's days.

One day, when she'd been living there two weeks, Jule found herself alone for the first time. Forrest and Immie had gone on a lunch date. There was a new restaurant Immie wanted to try.

Jule ate leftovers in front of the television and then went upstairs. She stood at the door of Immie's bedroom for a moment, looking in.

The bed was made. The table held books, a jar of hand cream, Forrest's eyeglass case, and an empty charger. Jule stepped in and opened a perfume bottle, put some on, and rubbed her wrists together.

In the closet hung a dress Imogen wore often. It was a dark green maxi, thin cotton, with a deep V in the front that made it impossible to wear a bra. Immie was flat-chested, so it didn't matter.

Without thinking, Jule pulled off her running shorts and then her bleached, frayed Stanford T-shirt. Then her bra.

She pulled Immie's dress over her head. She found a pair of sandals. Immie's collection of rings, eight of them in animal shapes, were on top of the dresser.

A full-length mirror in a wide silver frame leaned against one wall. Jule turned and squinted at herself. Her hair was in a ponytail, but other than that, in the low light of the room, she looked like Imogen. Mostly.

So this was what it felt like. To sit on Imogen's bed. To wear Imogen's fragrance and Imogen's rings.

Immie lay in this bed at night, next to Forrest, but he was replaceable. Immie put this cream on her hands, marked her reading with that bookmark. In the mornings, she opened her eyes and saw these blue-green sheets and that painting of the sea. This was what it felt like to know that this enormous house was hers, to never worry about money or survival, to feel loved by Gil and Patti.

To be so effortlessly, beautifully dressed.

"Excuse me?"

Immie stood in the doorway. She was wearing jean shorts and Forrest's hoodie. Her lips shone with a red gloss she didn't usually wear. She didn't look much like the Imogen in Jule's mind.

Shame washed through Jule's body, but she smiled. "I figured it would be okay," she said. "I needed a dress. This guy called, last minute."

"What guy?"

"The guy from Oak Bluffs, the one I talked to when I rode the carousel."

"When was that?"

"He texted just now and said did I want to meet him at the sculpture garden in half an hour."

"Whatever," said Immie. "Will you please get out of my clothes?"

Jule's face felt hot. "I didn't think you'd mind."

"Are you going to change?"

Jule pulled the top of Immie's green dress down and picked her bra up off the floor.

"Are those my rings, too?" said Immie.

"Yes." There was no pretending otherwise.

"Why would you wear my clothes?"

Jule stepped out of the dress and hung it back on the hanger. She put on the rest of her own clothes and replaced the rings on the dresser.

"I don't think you do have a guy waiting at the sculpture garden," said Immie.

"Think what you want to."

"What's going on?"

"I'm sorry I wore your clothes, and I won't do it again. Okay?"

"Okay." Imogen watched as Jule put the sandals in the closet and laced up her running shoes. "I have a question," she said as Jule made to walk past her into the hall.

Jule's face still burned. She didn't want to talk.

"Don't walk away," said Immie. "Answer me one thing, all right?"

"What is it?"

"Are you broke?" Imogen asked.

Yes. No. Yes. Jule hated how vulnerable the question made her feel.

"Dead," she finally said. "Yeah, I'm dead broke."

Immie put a hand over her mouth. "I didn't know."

And just like that, Jule had the upper hand. "It's all right," she said. "I can get a job. I mean, I haven't faced up to it like I need to."

"I should have realized." Immie sat down on the bed. "I knew about not going back to Stanford, and you said you fell out with your aunt, but I didn't put together how bad it was. Seeing you wear the same things over and over. Never buying groceries. Letting me pay."

Oh. So she needed to buy groceries. It was a code of behavior Jule hadn't understood until now. But all she said to Imogen was, "That's okay."

"No, it's not, Jule. I'm really sorry." Immie was silent for a moment. Then she said, "I think I've been assuming things about your life that I shouldn't assume. And I didn't ask you to tell me. I don't have very broad experience, I guess."

Jule shrugged. "You're lucky."

"Isaac was always telling me I had a narrow perspective. Anyway. Borrow anything you want."

"I'd feel strange now."

"Don't feel strange." Immie pulled open the closet. It was jammed with clothes. "I have more than I need."

She walked back to Jule. "Let me fix your hair. You've got bobby pins loose."

Jule's hair was long. Mostly she wore it pulled back tight. Now she bent her head forward, and Immie pinned up a couple of pieces on the neck that had come loose.

"You should cut it short," said Immie. "It'd look good on you. Not quite like mine. A little longer in the bangs, I think, and softer around the ears."

"No."

"I'll take you to my guy tomorrow, if you want," Immie pushed. "My treat."

Jule shook her head.

"Let me do something for you," said Immie. "You deserve it."

. . .

In Oak Bluffs the next day, Jule felt light, without the weight of her hair. It was nice having Imogen take care of her. Lending her a lip gloss after the cut. Taking her out to lunch at a restaurant with views of the harbor. After the meal they stepped into a vintage jewelry shop. "I want to see the most unusual ring you have for sale," Immie said.

The salesman bustled around and lined up six rings on a velvet tray. Imogen fingered them reverently. She selected a jade one in the shape of a viper, paid for it, and handed the blue velvet box to Jule. "This one is for you."

Jule opened the box immediately and slid the snake onto the ring finger of her right hand. "I'm too young to get married," she said. "Don't go getting ideas."

Immie laughed. "I love you," she said casually.

It was the first time Immie had used the word *love*.

The next day, Jule borrowed the car to pick up propane for the grill at the hardware store on the other side of the island. She bought some groceries, too. When she came back, Imogen and Forrest were naked, wrapped around each other in the swimming pool.

Jule stood on the inside of the screen door, staring.

The two of them looked so awkward, humping around. Forrest's long hair was wet and down around his shoulders. His glasses were at the edge of the pool, and his face looked dim and empty without them.

It seemed impossible. Jule was sure Imogen couldn't really love or want Forrest. He was only an idea of a boyfriend: a placeholder. Though he didn't know it, he was a temporary person, like the college kids and art students who came over for dinner and were never seen again. Forrest didn't hear Immie's secrets. He wasn't beloved. Jule had never believed Imogen could grab his face and kiss him and seem hungry for him and crazy about him, the way she was doing right now. She hadn't really believed Imogen would even be naked in front of him, so vulnerable.

Forrest saw her.

Jule started back, expecting him to yell, or to be embarrassed, but Forrest just said to Immie, "Your little friend is here," as if he were talking about a child.

Imogen turned her head and said, "Bye-bye, Jule. We'll see you later."

Jule turned and ran upstairs.

Hours later, Jule came downstairs. She heard a podcast playing in the kitchen, which was Imogen's usual habit when cooking, and she found Immie slicing zucchini for the grill.

"Do you need help?" Jule asked. She felt massively awkward. The fact of having witnessed that scene was excruciating. It might ruin everything.

"Sorry for the porno show," said Imogen lightly. "Do you mind cutting a red onion?"

Jule took an onion from the bowl.

"When I first got my flat in London," continued Imogen, "I had these two girlfriends from my program who were a couple. They had just come out, you know, being away from their families, and they were staying with me for August. I walked in on them absolutely *going at it* on the floor of the kitchen one day, like fully nude and yelling. I must have walked in at just a major effing moment, if you know what I mean. I thought, good Lord, are we ever going to be able to look each other in the face again? Like how could we all go out to the pub later, after this, and eat fish and chips? It just didn't seem possible, and I had this feeling like maybe I'd lost these two amazing friends just by coming home at the wrong time. But one of them was like, 'Oh, sorry for the porno show,' and we all burst out laughing and it was actually fine. So I figured I'd say that, too, if ever I got into the same kind of situation."

"You have an apartment in London?" Jule looked at the onion while she was peeling it.

"It was an investment," Immie said. "And kind of a

whim. I was in England on a summer program. My money person had advised me to put something in real estate, and I loved the city. This flat was the first place I looked at, an impulse buy in totally the wrong country, but I'm not sorry. It's in a very cute area: St. John's Wood." Immie pronounced it like *Sin Jahn's Wood*. "I had the most fun ever, decorating it with my friends. And we went around town and did tourist things. The Tower of London, the changing of the guard, the wax museum. We lived on digestive biscuits. It was before I learned to cook. You can borrow the place anytime. I never use it now."

"We should go together," said Jule.

"Oh, you'd be into it. The keys are right here. We could go tomorrow," Immie said, and patted the bag that sat on the kitchen counter. "And maybe we should. Can you imagine? Just you and me in London?"

Immie loved people who were passionate. She wanted them to love the music she loved, the flowers she gave them, the books she admired. She wanted them to care about the smell of a spice or the taste of a new kind of salt. She didn't mind disagreement, but she hated people who were apathetic and indecisive.

Jule read the two orphan books Immie had put on her bedside table, and everything else Immie brought home for her. She memorized wine labels, cheese labels, passages from novels, recipes. She was sweet with Forrest. She was scrappy yet willing to please, feminist yet feminine, full of rage yet friendly, articulate yet not dogmatic.

She realized that the manufacture of herself to please Imogen—it was like running, really. You simply powered through, mile after mile. Eventually you developed endurance. One day, you realized you loved it.

When Jule had been at the Vineyard house five weeks, Brooke Lannon showed up on Immie's porch. Jule opened the door.

Brooke walked in and threw her bags down on the couch. Her blue flannel shirt was threadbare and old, and her silky blond hair was up in a topknot. "Immie, you still exist, you witch," she said as Immie came into the living room. "All of Vassar thinks you're dead. Nobody believed me when I said you texted me last week." She turned to look at Forrest. "Is this the guy? Who . . . ?" She left a question mark in the air.

"This is *Forrest*," said Immie.

"Forrest!" said Brooke, shaking hands. "Okay, let's hug."

Forrest hugged awkwardly. "Nice to meet you."

"It is always nice to meet me," said Brooke. Then she pointed to Jule. "Who's this?"

"Don't be mean," said Immie.

"I'm being delightful," said Brooke. "Who are you?" This, to Jule.

Jule forced a smile and introduced herself. She hadn't known Brooke was coming. And Brooke clearly hadn't heard about Jule being there, either. "Imogen says you're her favorite person from Vassar."

"I'm everyone's favorite person from Vassar," said Brooke. "That's why I had to drop out. It was only two thousand people. I need a bigger audience."

She dragged her bags upstairs and made herself at home in the second-best guest room.

📅 **END OF JUNE, 2016**
📍 **MARTHA'S VINEYARD, MASSACHUSETTS**

Five weeks before Brooke arrived, on her seventh day on Martha's Vineyard, Jule splurged and took a tourist bus around the island. Most of the people on the bus were the kind who want to check off the sights on a list from a travel website. They were in family groups and couples, talking loudly.

The afternoon brought the tour to the Aquinnah lighthouse, in an area the guide explained was first inhabited by the Wampanoag Tribe of Gay Head and later, in the 1600s, by English colonists as well. The guide started talking about whaling as everyone poured off the bus to gaze at the lighthouse. From the lookout, they could also see the colored clay cliffs of Moshup Beach, but you couldn't get down to the water without a hot walk of about half a mile.

Jule wandered away from the lookout to the Aquinnah shops, a cluster of small ventures selling souvenirs, Wampanoag crafts, and snacks. She wandered in and out of the low buildings, idly touching necklaces and postcards.

Maybe she should stay forever on Martha's Vineyard.

She could get a job in a shop or a gym, spend her days by the sea, find a place to live. She could give up trying to do anything with herself, stop being ambitious. She could just accept the life that was on offer right now and be grateful for it. No one would mess with her. She didn't have to look for Imogen Sokoloff at all, if she didn't want to.

As Jule exited one shop, a young man stepped out of the place opposite. He was carrying a large canvas tote bag. He was about Jule's age. No, a little older. He was lean and narrow-waisted, not muscular at all, but graceful and loose-limbed, with a slightly curved nose and nice bone structure. His brown hair was tied up in a bun. He wore black cotton pants that were so long as to be shredded at the bottoms, flip-flops, and a T-shirt that read LARSEN'S FISH MARKET.

"I don't know why you want to go in there," he called to his companion, who was presumably still inside the shop. "There's not any point in buying things that have no use."

There was no reply.

"Immie! Come on. Let's go to the beach," the boy called.

And there she was.

Imogen Sokoloff. Her hair was cut short and pixie-ish now, blonder than in the pictures, but there was no question of her identity. She looked exactly like herself.

She walked out of the shop like it was nothing, like Jule hadn't been waiting for her and looking for her for days and days. She was lovely, but more than that, she was at ease. As if loveliness were effortless.

Jule half expected Imogen to recognize her, but that didn't happen.

"You're so fussy today," Immie said to the guy. "It's boring when you're fussy."

"You didn't even buy anything," he said. "I want to get to the beach."

"The beach isn't going anywhere," said Imogen, digging in her bag. "And I did buy something."

The guy sighed. "What?"

"It's for you," she said. She pulled out a small paper parcel and gave it to him. He pulled the tape off and lifted out a woven bracelet.

Jule expected the boyfriend would be irritated, but instead he grinned. He put the bracelet on and buried his face in Imogen's neck. "I love it," he said. "It's perfect."

"It's a trinket," she said. "You hate trinkets."

"But I like presents," he said.

"I know you do."

"Come on," he said. "The water should be warm." They walked down through the parking lot toward the path to the beach.

Jule looked back. The tour guide was waving at the crowd, gesturing for people to get back on the bus. It was scheduled to leave in five minutes.

She had no way to return to the hotel. Her phone was nearly out of battery and she didn't know if she could call a cab from this part of the island.

It didn't matter. She had found Imogen Sokoloff.

Jule let the bus leave without her.

4

One week earlier, a guard stopped Jule at airport security. "If you want to carry this bag on, miss, you have to put the toiletries in a clear plastic bag," the man told her. He had a flabby neck and wore a blue uniform. "Didn't you see the sign? Everything has to be three point four ounces."

The guard was going through Jule's suitcase wearing a pair of blue latex gloves. He took her shampoo, her conditioner, her sunblock, her body lotion. He threw them all in the trash.

"I'll send it through again now," he said, zipping the bag shut. "Should be okay. You wait here."

She waited. She tried to look as if she'd known how to pack liquids for air travel and had simply forgotten, but her ears grew hot. She was angry at the waste. She felt small and inexperienced.

The plane was cramped, with plasticky seats worn down by years of use, but Jule enjoyed the flight. The view was exciting. It was a cloudless day. The shoreline curved down the coast, brown and green.

Her hotel was opposite the harbor in Oak Bluffs. It was a Victorian building with white trim. Jule left her suitcase in the room and walked a few blocks to Circuit Avenue. The town was filled with vacationers. There were a couple of shops with nice clothing. Jule needed clothes; she had the Visa gift cards, and she knew what looked good on her, but she hesitated.

She watched the women as they walked by. They wore jeans or short cotton skirts and open-toe sandals. Faded colors and navy blue. Their bags were fabric, not leather. Their lipstick was nude and pink, never red. Some wore white pants and espadrilles. Their bras didn't show. They wore only the smallest earrings.

Jule took out her hoops and tucked them in her bag. She returned to the shops, where she bought a pair of boyfriend jeans, three cotton tank tops, a long flowing cardigan, espadrilles, and a white sundress. Then a shoulder bag made of canvas printed with gray flowers. She paid with the card and got cash from a machine.

Standing on the street corner, Jule transferred her ID and money, makeup and phone to the new bag. She called her phone's billing service and arranged payment with the Visa number. She called her roommate, Lita, and left a voice mail saying she was sorry.

At the hotel, Jule worked out, showered, and put on the white dress. She blew her hair out in loose waves. She needed to find Imogen, but it could wait until the next day.

She walked to an oyster bar that looked onto the harbor and asked for a lobster roll. When it arrived, it wasn't what she expected. It was nothing but lobster chunks in mayonnaise on a toasted hot dog bun. She had imagined it would be something more elegant.

She asked for a plate of french fries and ate those instead.

It was strange to walk through town with nothing she needed to do. Jule ended up at the carousel. It was indoors, in a dark old building that smelled of popcorn. A sign claimed that Flying Horses was "America's Oldest Carousel."

She bought a ticket. It wasn't crowded, just a few kids and their older siblings. Parents were looking at their phones in the waiting area. The music was old-fashioned. Jule chose an outside horse.

As the ride started, she noticed the guy sitting on the pony next to her. He was wiry, with developed deltoids and lats: possibly a rock climber, definitely not a weight-room guy. Some white and some Asian heritage, Jule guessed. He had thick black hair, a little too long. He looked like he had been out in the sun. "I'm feeling like a loser right now," he told her as the carousel started moving. "Like this was a crazy bad idea." His accent was general American.

Jule matched it. "How come?"

"Nausea. It hit me right away, as soon as we started

moving. Blech. Also I'm the only person on this thing who's over the age of ten."

"Besides me."

"Besides you. I rode this carousel once when I was a kid. My family came here on a vacation. Today I was waiting for the ferry and I had an hour to kill, so I thought—why not? For old times' sake." He rubbed his forehead with one hand. "Why are you on here? Do you have a little brother or sister somewhere?"

Jule shook her head. "I like rides."

He reached across the space between them and held out his hand. "I'm Paolo Santos. You?"

She shook awkwardly, since both their horses were moving.

This guy was leaving the island. Jule was only talking to him for a minute or two; then she'd never see him again. It didn't make much sense; it was an impulse—but she lied. "Imogen Sokoloff."

The name felt good to say. It would be nice, after all, to be Imogen.

"Oh, you're *Imogen Sokoloff*?" Paolo threw his head back, laughing and raising his soft eyebrows. "I should have guessed. I heard you might be on the Vineyard."

"You knew I was here?"

"I should explain. I gave you a fake name. I'm really sorry, that probably seems crazy. Just a fake last name. It's really Paolo. But not really Santos."

"Oh."

"I'm sorry." He rubbed his forehead again. "It was a strange thing to do, but I figured we were only talking to each other for the next couple minutes. Sometimes when I'm traveling I like to be someone else."

"That's okay."

"I'm Paolo Vallarta-Bellstone. My dad, Stuart, went to school with your father. I'm sure you've met him."

Jule raised her eyebrows. She had heard of Stuart Bellstone. He was a big financial guy recently sent to prison for what the news sites called "the D and G trading scandal." His picture had been all over the news two months ago when the trial ended.

"I've played golf with your father and my dad a number of times," Paolo went on. "Before Gil got sick. He always talked about you. You went to Greenbriar and then you started at—Vassar, was it?"

"Yes, but I dropped out after fall term," said Jule.

"How come?"

"That's a long and boring story."

"Come on. You'll distract me from my nausea and then I won't be sick on you. It'll be a win all around."

"My dad would say I got in with party people and didn't work up to my potential in my first semester," said Jule.

Paolo laughed. "Sounds like him. What would *you* say?"

"I would say . . . that I wanted a different life than the one that was supposed to be my lot," said Jule slowly. "Coming here was a way to get it."

The carousel slowed to a stop. They got off their horses and walked out. Paolo grabbed a large backpack from a corner where he'd stashed it. "You wanna go get ice cream?" he asked. "I know the best ice cream place on the island."

They walked along to a little shop. They argued about

hot fudge versus butterscotch topping and then agreed that both at once would solve everything. Paolo said, "It's so funny, your being here right now. I feel like we nearly met a million times."

"How did you know I was on Martha's Vineyard?"

Paolo ate a spoonful of ice cream. "You're a little bit famous, Imogen, leaving school and going missing—then turning up here. Your dad asked me to call you when I was on the island, to be honest."

"He did not."

"Yeah. He emailed me. See? I called your number six days ago." He pulled out an iPhone and showed her the recent calls.

"That's a little creepy."

"No, it's not," said Paolo. "Gil wants to know how you are, is all. He said you haven't been picking up your phone, you'd left school, and you were out on the Vineyard. If I saw you, I should report back that you're okay. He wanted me to tell you he's having an operation."

"I know he's having an operation. I was just in the city with him."

"So my efforts were wasted," said Paolo, shrugging. "Won't be the first time."

They walked back to the harbor and looked at boats. Paolo talked about traveling to escape his father's shattered reputation and the family fallout. He had graduated from college in May and was thinking about going to medical school, but he wanted to see the world before committing. He was going now to spend a night in Boston before getting on a plane to Madrid. He and a friend would be backpacking for a year or more—Europe first, then Asia, ending up in the Philippines.

His ferry was boarding. Paolo kissed Jule quickly on the lips before he left. He was gentle and confident, not pushy. His lips were a little sticky from the butterscotch sauce.

Jule was surprised at the kiss. She didn't want him to touch her. She didn't want anyone to touch her, ever. But when Paolo's full, soft lips brushed hers, she liked it.

She reached her hand to his neck, pulled him toward her, and kissed him again. He was a beautiful guy, she thought. Not all dominant and sweaty. Not all grabby and violent. Not condescending. Not all flattery and gold chains, either. His kiss was so gentle she had to lean in to feel it all the way.

She wished she had told him her real name.

"Can I call you?" he asked. "Again, I mean? Not for your father's sake."

No, no.

Paolo couldn't call Imogen's phone again. If he did, he'd realize it wasn't Imogen he'd met. "You'd better not," said Jule.

"Why not? I'll be in Madrid, and then wherever, but we could—we could just talk, now and then. About hot fudge and butterscotch, maybe. Or your new life."

"I'm attached," Jule said, to make him be quiet.

Paolo's face fell. "Oh, you are. Of course you are. Well, you have my number anyhow," he said. "I left a message a while back. It's a 646 number. So you can ping me if you detach—unattach, whatever it is. Okay?"

"I'm not going to call you," said Jule. "But thank you for the ice cream."

He looked hurt, briefly. But then he smiled. "Anytime, Imogen."

He shouldered his backpack, and was gone.

Jule watched his ferry pull away from the dock. Then she took off her espadrilles and walked down onto the sand. She stood with her feet in the water. She felt Imogen Sokoloff would have done that, would have savored the slight feeling of sadness and the beauty of the harbor view while holding the skirt of her pretty white dress above her knees.

3

A week before going to Martha's Vineyard, Jule stood with Patti Sokoloff on a deck overlooking Central Park. The sun had set. The park stretched out, a dark rectangle ringed by the city lights.

"I feel like Spider-Man," Jule blurted. "He looks out over the city at night."

Patti nodded. Her hair fell in big, professional curls on her shoulders, and she wore a long cardigan over a cream-colored dress and pretty, flat sandals. Her feet looked old and had Band-Aids on the heels and toes. "Immie had a boyfriend who came over here for a party once," she told Jule. "He said the same thing about the view. Well, Batman, he said. But it's the same idea."

"They're not the same."

"Okay, but they're both orphans," said Patti. "Batman lost his parents very early. And so did Spider-Man. He lives with his aunt."

"You read comics?"

"Never. But I proofread Immie's college essay about six

times. She said Spider-Man and Batman are descended from all the orphans in these Victorian novels she likes. Immie's really into Victorian novels, did you know that? It's a thing she hangs her identity on. You know, some people define themselves as athletes, social justice warriors, theater kids. Immie defines herself as a Victorian novel reader.

"She isn't the best student," Patti went on, "but she's into literature. For the college essay, she wrote that in these stories, being orphaned is a precondition for the making of a hero. She also said those comic book heroes aren't simple heroes, but 'complicated ones who make moral compromises in the same tradition as the orphans in Victorian narratives.' I think those might be the exact words from her paper."

"I used to read comics in high school," said Jule. "But there was no time at Stanford."

"Gil grew up with comic books, but I didn't, and neither did Immie, really. The superheroes were just her introduction, to point out why the older books were important for today's readers. She got most of the Batman stuff from that boyfriend I mentioned."

They turned to go inside. The Sokoloff penthouse was dramatic and modern but cluttered with piles of books, magazines, and keepsakes. The floors were white wood, everywhere. A cook was at work in the kitchen, where the breakfast table was piled with junk mail, pill bottles, and tissue packets. The living room was centered on two huge leather couches. Next to one of them was a breathing machine.

Gil Sokoloff didn't get up as Patti led Jule into the room. He was only in his fifties, but pain lines creased the sides of his mouth, and the flesh of his neck hung baggy. The shape of his face was Eastern European, and he had a thick mass of curly gray hair. He wore sweatpants and a gray T-shirt. His cheeks and nose were speckled with broken blood vessels. He leaned forward slowly, as if moving hurt him, and shook Jule's hand, then introduced two tubby white dogs: Snowball and Snowman. He introduced Imogen's three cats, too.

They went straight in to dinner in a formal dining room, Gil shuffling and Patti walking slowly next to him. The cook brought out bowls and platters, then left them alone. They ate tiny lamb chops and a mushroom risotto. Gil asked for his oxygen tank halfway through the meal.

During the cheese course, they talked about the dogs, which were new. "They've ruined our lives," said Patti. "They poo constantly. Gil lets them do it on the deck. Can you believe that? I walk out there in the morning and there's a stinky dog poo."

"They whine to go out there before you're up," said Gil, unrepentant. He moved the oxygen mask to the side so he could talk. "What am I supposed to do?"

"Then we have to spray it with bleach cleaner. There are little bleach spots all over the wood," said Patti. "It's foul. Still, that's what you do when you love an animal. You let them poo on your deck, I suppose."

"Imogen was always bringing home stray cats," said Gil. "It was another kitten every couple months, in high school."

"Some of them didn't make it," said Patti. "She would find them on the street and they had kitty bronchitis or some other plague. They would die a tiny sad death, and Immie would burst her heart every time. Then she went to Vassar and we were left with these guys." Patti stroked a cat that was wandering under the dinner table. "Nothing but trouble, and proud of it."

Like any Greenbriar "old girl," Patti had stories of her school days. "We had to wear stockings or knee socks with our uniforms, year-round," she said. "And come summer, we were so uncomfortable. In high school—this was in the late seventies—some of us went without underwear, just to stay cool. Knee socks with no underwear!" She patted Jule's shoulder. "You and Immie were lucky the uniforms changed. Did you do music at Greenbriar? You sounded so passionate about Gershwin the other day."

"A little."

"Do you remember the winter concert?"

"Sure."

"I can just see you and Imogen, standing together. You were the tiniest girls in the ninth grade. You all sang carols, and the Caraway girl had the solo. Do you remember?"

"Of course."

"They lit the ballroom up for the holidays, with the tree in that one corner. They had a menorah, too, of course, but they didn't really mean it," said Patti. "Oh, damn. I'm going to get teary, thinking about Immie in that blue velvet dress. I bought her a holiday dress for that concert, royal blue with darts down the front."

"Immie rescued me on my first day at Greenbriar," said Jule. "Someone knocked into me in the cafeteria line, and spaghetti sauce splashed all over my shirt. There I stood, looking at all those glossy girls in clean clothes. Everyone knew each other from the lower school already." The story flowed easily. Patti and Gil were good listeners. "How could I sit down at anyone's table when I had sauce, like blood, all over me?"

"Oh, sweet potato."

"Immie came striding over. She took my tray out of my hands. She introduced me to all her friends and pretended she couldn't see the mess all over my shirt, so they pretended they couldn't see it, either. And that was that," said Jule. "She was one of my favorite people, but we never kept up after I moved away."

Later, in the living room, Gil settled into the couch with his oxygen tubes in his nose. Patti brought out a thick photo album made of gilded paper. "You'll let me show you pictures, won't you?"

They looked through old photographs. Jule found Imogen exceptionally pretty—short and a little impish. She had light hair and fat dimpled cheeks that later became high cheekbones. In many of the pictures she was displayed in front of some attractive destination. "We went to Paris," Patti said, or "We visited a farm," or "That's the oldest carousel in America." Immie wore twirly skirts and stripy leggings. Her hair was long in most pictures, and a little wild. In later pictures, she had braces on her teeth.

"She never had any adopted friends after you left Greenbriar," said Patti. "I always felt we failed her that way." Patti leaned forward. "Did you have that? A community of families like yours?"

Jule took a deep breath. "I didn't have that."

"Do you feel your parents failed you?" asked Patti.

"Yes," said Jule. "My parents did fail me."

"I think so often that I should have raised Immie differently. Done more. Talked more about the difficult things." Patti rambled on, but Jule didn't hear her.

Julietta's parents had died when she was eight. Her mother passed away from a long and gruesome illness. Shortly afterward, her father bled himself out, naked in a bathtub.

Julietta had been raised by another person, that aunt, in a home that was not a home.

No. She would not think about it anymore. She was erasing it now.

She was writing a new story for herself, an origin story. In this version, the living room was trashed. In the dark of night. Yes, that was it. The story wasn't finished yet, but she ran it through as well as she could. She saw her parents in the circle of light created by the streetlamp, dead in the grass with the blood pooling black beneath them.

"We need to get to the point," said Gil, wheezing. "The girl doesn't have all night."

Patti nodded. "What I haven't told you, and why we asked you here, is that Imogen dropped out of Vassar after first term."

"We think she got in with party people," said Gil. "She didn't work up to her potential in her classes."

"Well, she never did love school," said Patti. "Not the way you obviously love Stanford, Jule. Anyway, she left Vassar without even telling us, and it was a month before she even got in touch. We were so worried."

"*You* were so worried," said Gil. He leaned forward. "I was just angry. Imogen is irresponsible. She loses her phone or forgets to turn it on. She's not good with calling, texting, any of that."

"It turns out she went to Martha's Vineyard," said Patti. "We used to go there all the time as a family, and she ran away there, apparently. She told us she rented a place, but she didn't give us an address, or even a town."

"Why don't you go see her?" asked Jule.

"I can't go anywhere," said Gil.

"He has kidney dialysis every other day. It's exhausting. And he has to have procedures," said Patti.

"All my insides are coming out soon," said Gil. "I'm going to be carrying them around in a bag."

Patti bent and kissed him on the cheek. "So we had the idea that maybe you'd like to go over, Jule. To the Vineyard. We thought of hiring a detective—"

"*You* thought about it," said Gil. "A ridiculous idea."

"We did ask some college friends of hers, but they didn't want to interfere," said Patti.

"What do you want me to do?" Jule asked.

"Make sure she's okay. Don't tell her we sent you, but text us so we know how things are going," said Patti. "Try to convince her to come home."

"You're not working this summer, are you?" asked Gil. "No internship, nothing like that?"

"No," said Jule. "I don't have a job."

"Naturally we'll pay your expenses to the Vineyard," said Gil. "We can give you gift cards for a couple thousand dollars, and we'll pay for a hotel."

The Sokoloffs were so trusting. So kind. So stupid. The cats, the dogs who pooped on the deck, Gil's oxygen tank, the albums full of pictures, the worry about Imogen, the interference, even; the clutter, the lamb chops, the chatty way they talked, everything was wonderful.

"I'd be glad to help you out," Jule told them.

Jule took the subway back to her apartment. She opened her computer, did a search, and ordered a red Stanford University T-shirt.

When it arrived a couple of days later, she yanked the neck until it was loose and sprayed the bottom edge with bleach cleaner to make a stain.

She washed it repeatedly until it was soft and seemed old.

One day before dinner at Patti's, Jule stood on a street in upper Manhattan, holding an address on a scrap of paper. It was ten a.m. She wore a flattering black cotton dress with a square neckline. Her heels were black, too, with a sling back and a sharply pointed toe. They were too small for her. She had a pair of running shoes in her bag. She had made up her face in a style she thought of as college girl. Her hair was in a bun.

The Greenbriar School occupied a number of renovated mansions along Fifth Avenue at Eighty-Second Street. The stone facade of the upper school, where Jule was to work, stood five stories high. A curving set of steps led to statues by the entrance. Big double doors. It looked like a place where you could get a highly unusual education.

"Event is in the ballroom," said the guard as Jule went in. "Staircase on your right to the second floor."

The entryway had marble floors. A sign to the left read MAIN OFFICE, and a corkboard next to it listed the graduating seniors' college destinations: Yale, Penn, Harvard, Brown,

Williams, Princeton, Swarthmore, Dartmouth, Stanford. They seemed like fictional locations to Jule. It was strange to see them written down like a poem, each name on its own line, and each word speaking an immensity.

At the top of the stairs, the hall opened into a ballroom. A commanding woman in a red jacket came forward with a hand outstretched. "Catering? Welcome to Greenbriar," she said. "So glad you could help us today. I'm Mary Alice McIntosh, the fund-raising chair."

"Good to meet you. I'm Lita Kruschala."

"Greenbriar was a pioneer in education for women beginning in 1926," McIntosh said. "We occupy three beaux arts mansions that were originally private homes. The buildings are landmarked, and our donors today are philanthropists and supporters of education for girls."

"It's an all-girls school?"

McIntosh handed Jule a ruffled black apron. "Studies show that in single-sex schools, girls take more nontraditional courses like advanced science. They worry less about how they look, they're more competitive, and they have higher self-esteem." She recited it like a speech she had given a thousand times. "Today we expect a hundred guests here for music and passed hors d'oeuvres. Then a sit-down lunch upstairs in the parlors on the third floor." McIntosh walked Jule into the ballroom, where tall tables were being covered with white cloths. "The girls come here for assembly on Mondays and Fridays, and in the middle of the week we use it for yoga and visiting speakers."

Oil paintings decorated the walls of the ballroom. There

was a strong smell of furniture polish. Three chandeliers hung from the ceiling, and a grand piano stood in one corner. It was hard to believe people went to school here.

McIntosh pointed Jule to the catering supervisor, and Jule gave Lita's name. She fastened the apron over her dress. The supervisor set her to folding napkins, but as soon as he turned his back, Jule went across the hall and peeked into a classroom.

It was lined with books. There was a Smartboard against one wall and a row of computers against another, but the center of the room felt old. There was a rich red rug on the floor. Heavy chairs circled a wide old table. On the chalkboard, the teacher had written:

> Free write, 10 minutes:
> "The important thing is this: to be able at any moment to sacrifice what we are for what we could become."
> —Charles Du Bos

Jule touched the edge of the table. She would sit at that seat, there, she decided. That would be her regular place, with her back to the light from the window and her eye on the door. She'd argue over the Du Bos quote with the other students. The teacher, a woman in black, would loom over them, not threatening but inspiring. She'd push them to excel. She'd believe that her girls were the future.

There was a cough. The catering supervisor stood in the room with Jule. He pointed at the door. Jule followed him back to the pile of napkins and began to fold.

A pianist arrived in the ballroom, bustling. He was scrawny, freckly-white, and redheaded. His wrists stuck too far out of his jacket. He unpacked sheet music, checked his phone for a minute or two, and then began to play. The music was punchy and somehow classy. It made the room feel bright, as if the party had already started. When she finished the napkins, Jule walked over. "What's the song?"

"Gershwin," the pianist said with disdain. "It's an all-Gershwin luncheon. People with money love Gershwin."

"You don't?"

He shrugged while still playing. "It pays the rent."

"I thought people who played grand pianos already had money."

"We have debt, usually."

"So who's Gershwin?"

"Who *was* Gershwin?" The pianist stopped what he was playing and started something new. Jule watched his hands run over the keyboard and recognized the song. *Summertime, and the livin' is easy.*

"I know that one," she said. "He's dead?"

"Long ago. He was from the twenties and thirties. He was a first-gen immigrant; his dad was a shoemaker. He came up through the Yiddish theater scene and started out writing poppy jazz songs for quick money, then did music for the movies. Then, later, classical and opera. So he ended up high-class, but he came from nothing."

How amazing to be able to play an instrument, Jule thought. Whatever happened to you, whatever else went on in your life, you could look down at your hands and think, *I play the piano.* You'd always know that about yourself.

It was like being able to fight, she realized. And being able to change accents. They were powers that lived in your body. They would never leave you, no matter how you looked, no matter who loved or didn't love you.

An hour later, the catering supervisor tapped Jule on the shoulder. "You have cocktail sauce on you, Lita," he said. "Sour cream, too. Go fix yourself up and I'll give you another apron."

Jule looked down. She took off the apron and handed it over.

There was someone using the bathroom nearest the ballroom, so Jule climbed the stone staircase to the third floor. She glimpsed a pair of elegant parlors. The tables were decorated with bursts of pink flowers. Guests shook hands and suffered introductions.

The women's room had a lounge. It was papered in green and gold and had a small, ornate couch inside. Jule walked through and opened the door to the toilet. There, she took Lita's shoes off. Her feet were swollen at the toes and bleeding at the heels. She blotted them with a wet paper towel. Then she wiped at the dress until it was clean.

She stepped back into the lounge barefoot to find a woman in her fifties sitting on the couch. The woman was pretty in an upper-Manhattan way: tan skin with careful rouge and dyed brown hair. She wore a green silk dress that made her seem as if she belonged on that green velvet couch with that green-and-gold wallpaper. She had bare legs and was applying bandages to her blistered toes. A pair of strappy heels lay on the floor.

"The heat makes my feet swell," the woman said, "and then there's no end to the suffering. Am I right?"

Jule answered in an accent that matched the woman's: general American. "Can you spare a Band-Aid?"

"I have a whole box," the woman replied. She dug into a large handbag and produced it. "I came prepared." Her finger- and toenails were polished a shade of pale pink.

"Thank you." Jule sat down beside her and doctored her own feet.

"You don't remember me, do you?" said the woman.

"I—"

"Don't worry. I remember *you*. You and my daughter Immie always looked like two peas in a pod, in your uniforms. Both so petite, and with those cute freckles across the nose."

Jule blinked.

The woman smiled. "I'm Imogen Sokoloff's mother, sweet potato. Call me Patti. You came to Imogen's birthday party freshman year, remember? The sleepover where we made cake pops. And you and Immie used to go shopping down in SoHo. Oh, do you remember, we took you to *Coppelia* at American Ballet Theatre?"

"Of course," said Jule. "I'm sorry I didn't recognize you right away."

"No worries," said Patti. "I've forgotten your name, I have to tell you, though I never forget a face. And you had that fun blue hair."

"It's Jule."

"Of course. It was so cool that you and Immie were such friends, that first year of high school. After you left, she went around with these kids from Dalton. I never liked

241

them half as well. There are only a few recent grads here at the benefit, I think. Maybe no one you know? It's all old girls like me."

"They sent me the invitation and I came for the Gershwin," said Jule. "And to see the place after being away."

"How great that you appreciate Gershwin," said Patti. "In my teens I was all punk rock, and in my twenties it was Madonna and whoever. Where are you in college?"

A beat. A choice. Jule threw her Band-Aid wrappers in the trash.

"Stanford," she answered. "But I'm not sure I'm going back in the fall." She rolled her eyes comically. "I'm in a war with the financial aid office." Everything she told Patti felt delicious in her mouth, like melting caramel.

"That's unpleasant," said Patti. "I thought they had great financial aid there."

"They do, generally," said Jule. "But not for me."

Patti looked at Jule seriously. "I think it will work out. Looking at you, I can tell you're not going to let any doors shut in your face. Listen, do you have a summer job, an internship, something like that?"

"Not yet."

"Then I have an idea I want to talk to you about. Just a crazy thought I'm having, but you might like it." She took a cream-colored card out of her handbag and handed it to Jule. It had a Fifth Avenue address. "I have to get home to my husband now. He's not well. But why don't you come to dinner at our place tomorrow night? I know Gil will be thrilled to meet one of Immie's old friends."

"Thanks, I'd love to."

"Seven o'clock?"

"I'll be there," said Jule. "Now, do we dare put our shoes on?"

"Oh, I guess we have to," said Patti. "It's very hard to be a woman sometimes."

📅 **FIRST WEEK OF JUNE, 2016**

📍 **NEW YORK CITY**

Sixteen hours earlier, at eight p.m., Jule got out of the subway in a dodgy Brooklyn neighborhood. She'd spent the day looking for work. It was the fourth time in a row she'd worn her best dress.

No luck.

Her apartment was a flight up from a bodega with a dingy yellow awning: the Joyful Food Mart. It was a Friday night, and guys clustered on the street corner, talking loudly. The trash cans on the sidewalks overflowed.

Jule had only lived here for four weeks. She shared the place with a roommate, Lita Kruschala. Today the rent was due and she had no way to pay it.

She wasn't close with Lita. They had met when Jule answered a listing she'd found online. Before that she had been staying at a youth hostel. She'd used the public library Internet to look for apartment shares.

When she went to see the rental, Lita was offering the living room of an apartment as a bedroom. It was sectioned off from the kitchen with a curtain. Lita told Jule her sister had recently moved back home to Poland. Lita preferred to stay on in America. She cleaned apartments and worked for a catering company, both for cash. She wasn't legal to work in the US. She took English classes at the YMCA.

Jule told Lita she had a job as a personal trainer. That was what she'd done back in Florida, and Lita believed her. Jule had paid a month's rent, cash, in advance. Lita didn't ask for ID. Jule never spoke the name Julietta.

Some evenings, Lita's friends were over, speaking Polish and smoking cigarettes. They made stewed meats and boiled potatoes in the kitchen. Those nights, Jule put on headphones and curled up on her bed, practicing her accents from tutorials online. Sometimes Lita stepped into Jule's room with a bowl of stew and gave it over without saying anything.

Jule had arrived in New York by bus. After the boy and the blue slush, after the strappy heeled shoe and the blood on the sidewalk, after that boy had fallen, Julietta West Williams had disappeared from the state of Alabama. She'd left school, too. She was seventeen and didn't have to finish her education. No law said she had to.

She might have been okay staying put. That boy did live, and he never said a word. But then, if she'd stayed in town, he might have spoken up. Or he might have retaliated.

Pensacola, Florida, was only a couple hundred miles away. Jule got hired to work for cash at a storefront gym in a strip mall. The owners didn't ask their staff to be certified trainers. They jacked their boys up on steroids, and everything was less than legit.

Julietta put guys through workouts every day. Bouncers,

thugs, bodyguards, even a few cops. She worked there six months and put on muscle. The boss owned a martial arts place a mile away, and he let her take classes there for free. Julietta rented a week-by-week motel room with a kitchenette. She bought a laptop and a phone, but other than that, she saved her money.

Lunch hours, she often walked a ways down the road to the shopping mall. It was a high-end place with fountains and flagship stores. Julietta read in the airy bookshop, window-shopped thousand-dollar dresses, and tried on makeup in the department store. She learned the names of the classiest brands. She reinvented herself with powders, creams, and glosses. Her face looked one way one day, another way another. She never spent a cent.

That was how she'd met Neil. Neil was a slim guy in a butter-colored leather jacket. Now and then he spent an afternoon hanging around the makeup counters, talking to girls. He wore custom Nikes and spoke with a Southern accent. He couldn't have been older than twenty-five, and he had a white baby face with ruddy cheeks, sideburns, and a gold cross around his neck. The type of guy who was too loud in the movie theater and always bought a big popcorn.

"Neil what?" Julietta had asked.

"I don't use my last name," he answered. "It isn't as pretty as me."

Neil was in business. That was what he said when she asked what he was doing at the makeup counters: "I'm in business."

She wondered where that phrase came from. Was it a Pensacola phrase, or from somewhere else?

She knew what he meant.

"You could earn a lot more than you do now, working for me. I'd treat you so nice," Neil told her. It was the third day she'd talked to him. "What are you doing for money, pretty baby? I can see you're not spending any."

"Don't call me pretty baby."

"What? You're gorgeous."

"Do you seriously get girls to like you, calling them that?"

He shrugged and laughed. "Yeah, I do."

"You got some stupid girls, then."

"I have nice girls, that's what I have. They would show you how it goes. The work ain't hard."

"Right."

"You'd stay clean. You could get some pretty clothes. Sleep late every morning."

Julietta had blown him off that day, but Neil had been back around the makeup counters a week later. That time, he asked so politely that she let him buy her a burrito from a fast-food place in the mall. They sat at a dinky table by a pool of water.

"Guys like women with muscles, you know," Neil said. "Not everyone, but a lot of guys. Those types like to be bossed around. They want a girl built like you, who won't let them call her *pretty baby*. Do you know what I mean? I can get you very good money from a certain type of guy. Very, very good money."

"I'm not walking the streets," she told him.

"It's not the streets, newbie. It's a group of apartments with a doorman and an elevator. Jacuzzi bathtubs. I've got a guard who patrols the hall, keeps everybody safe. Listen, you've got it tough right now. I can tell, 'cause I've been there. I came from nothing, and I worked like hell to get a better life. You're a smart-mouth girl; a beautiful, unusual girl. You've got a bangin' body that's nonstop muscle, and I believe you deserve better than what you got going on. That's all."

Julietta listened.

He was saying what she felt. He understood her.

"Where you from, Julietta?"

"Alabama."

"You sound like you're from up north."

"I lost my accent."

"What?"

"I replaced it."

"How?"

The guys at the gym where Julietta worked were old. They only wanted to talk about reps and miles, weights and dosages. And they were the only people she ever talked to. Neil, at least, was young. "When I was nine," she told him, "one day I'd had—let's call it a bad day. Teacher telling us to be quiet. Yelling at *me* to be quiet. 'Shut up, little girl, you've said enough.' 'Stop, little girl, don't hit, use your words'— and *shut up* at the same time. They squash you. They want you to be small and silent. *Good* was just another word for *don't fight back.*"

Neil nodded. "I always got called out for being loud."

"One day, no one came to pick me up at school. Just— nobody came. The people in the office called and called my house, but no one picked up. This after-school teacher called

Miss Kayla, she drove me home. It was already dark out. I barely knew her. I got in her car because she had pretty hair. Yeah, stupid, to get in a stranger's car, I know. But she was a teacher. She gave me a box of Tic Tacs. While she was driving, she talked and talked, to cheer me up, you know? And she was from Canada. I don't know where in Canada, but she had an accent."

Neil nodded.

"I started imitating her," Julietta went on. "I was curious why she talked like that. She said *gaz* instead of gas. *Aboot* instead of about. That's called Canadian rising, by the way. It's a vowel shift. And I made Miss Kayla laugh, doing the accent. She told me I was a good mimic. Then we got to my house and she walked me to the door."

"Then what?"

"Someone was home all that time."

"Dang."

"Yeah. She was watching TV. She hadn't thought to come get me. Or she couldn't. I don't know. It was messed up, either way. She hadn't bothered to pick up the stupid phone, all those times the school called. I pushed the door open and walked in. I said, 'Where were you?' and she said, 'Be quiet, don't you see I got the TV on?' And I said, 'Why didn't you pick up the phone?' and she said, 'I told you to be quiet.' Just another *shut up and don't fight back.* So I got myself a bowl of dry cereal for dinner and watched the TV next to her. We had been watching for an hour or more when this idea hit me."

"What?"

"TV gives you an education in how to talk. Newscasters, rich people, doctors on those medical dramas. None of them talked the way I did. But they all talked like each other."

"I guess."

"It's true. I figured: learn to talk *that* way, and maybe you don't get told to shut up so much."

"You taught yourself?"

"I learned general American first. That's the one on TV. But now I do Boston, Brooklyn, West Coast, Lowland Southern, Central Canadian, BBC English, Irish, Scottish, South African."

"You want to be an actress. That it?"

Julietta shook her head. "I've got better things in mind."

"World domination, then."

"Something like that. I gotta figure it out."

"You could definitely be an actress," Neil said, grinning. "In fact, I bet you'll be in the movies. A year from now I'll be like, wow. That girl Julietta used to stand at the Chanel counter and cake on free makeup. That girl let me talk to her every now and then."

"Thanks."

"You need to get some nice clothes, Miss Julietta. You got to meet some big-money guys who'll buy you jewelry and pretty dresses. Talking like the television is one thing, but right now, it's all tracksuit, gym shoes, cheap-looking hair. You'll never get anywhere like that."

"I don't want to sell what you're selling."

"Let me hear you talk Brooklyn," said Neil.

"My lunch hour is over." She stood up.

"Come on. Irish, then."

"No."

"Well, you ever want a better job than the one you got, here's my number," Neil said, pulling a card out of his pocket. The card was black and had a cell number in silver writing.

"I'm leaving now."

Neil raised his Coke as if in a toast.

Julietta laughed as she walked away.

Neil made her feel pretty. He was a good listener.

The next morning she packed her bags and got on a bus to New York City. She was afraid of what she might become if she waited any longer.

Now Jule's rent was due. She'd been eating supermarket ramen. She had only five bucks in her wallet.

No gym in New York City would hire an unlicensed trainer. She didn't have a high school degree. She had no references because she'd ditched out on her first and only job. Gyms would pay the best, she'd figured, and she'd get a little saved and then look for something that would move her up in the world. Then, when none of them would hire her, she'd tried cosmetics counters, other retail jobs, nanny jobs, waiting tables, any opening listed. She'd been out looking every day, all day. There was nothing to show for it.

She stopped into the Joyful Food Mart below her apartment. It was busy inside. People getting off work bought boxes of pasta and cans of beans, or they played their numbers in the lottery. Jule bought a cup of vanilla pudding for a dollar and took a plastic spoon. She ate the pudding for dinner as she walked upstairs to the apartment she shared with Lita.

The apartment was dark. Jule was relieved. Lita had turned in early or was out late. In any case, Jule didn't have to make excuses for not having the rent.

Next morning, Lita didn't come out of her bedroom. Usually, she was up by seven on a Saturday to work her catering job. At eight, Jule knocked. "You okay?"

"I am dead," Lita called through the door.

Jule peeked in. "You have work today, right?"

"At ten. But I've been throwing up all night long. I mixed my cocktails."

"You need some water?"

Lita moaned.

"You want me to go to your job?" asked Jule, the idea dawning.

"I don't think so," said Lita. "Do you even know how to work catering?"

"Sure."

"If I don't show up, they'll fire me," said Lita.

"So let me go," said Jule. "We'll both come out good."

Lita swung her legs off the edge of the bed and clutched the side table, looking queasy. "Yeah. Okay."

"Really?"

"Just—tell them you're me."

"I look nothing like you."

"Doesn't matter. They got a new supervisor. He won't know the difference. It's a big operation. The important thing is, get my name checked off on the grid."

"Got it."

"And make sure the guy pays before you leave. Twenty an hour, cash, plus you'll get tips."

"I keep the money?"

"Half of it," said Lita. "It's my job, after all."

"Three-quarters," said Jule.

"Fine." Lita checked her phone and wrote down the info on a piece of paper. "Greenbriar School on the Upper East Side. You have to get the bus to the train, and then change to the subway."

"What's the event?"

"Party for donors to the school." Lita lay back down in the bed, moving as if she feared jostling her head. "I should not drink again, ever. Oh, you gotta wear a black dress."

"I don't have anything."

Lita sighed. "Take one from my closet. They'll give you an apron. No, not the one with the lace. That's dry-clean. Take a cotton one."

"I need shoes, too."

"God, Jule."

"Sorry."

"Take the heels. You'll get better tips."

Jule squeezed her feet into the heels. They were too small, but she'd manage. "Thanks."

"Bring half the tip money home to me, too," said Lita. "Those are my good shoes."

Jule had never worn a dress this nice. It was heavy cotton, a day dress with a square neck and a full skirt. She was surprised Lita had such a thing, but Lita said she got it for cheap at a resale shop.

Jule stepped onto the street in the dress and her running shoes, Lita's heels in her bag. The smell of New York City in the heat of early summer floated in the thick air around her: garbage, poverty, ambition.

She decided to walk across the Brooklyn Bridge. She could get the subway from the Manhattan side and wouldn't have to transfer.

The sun sparkled as she set out. The stone towers loomed. Jule could see boats in the harbor, leaving trails through the water. Lady Liberty was strong and bright.

It was strange how someone else's dress made her feel new. This sensation of being someone else, of changing into someone else, of being beautiful and young and crossing this famous bridge to something big—it was why Jule had come to New York.

She had never felt that possibility stretch out in front of her until this morning.

19

A little more than a year later, in the Cabo Inn, at five a.m., Jule stumbled to the bathroom, splashed water on her face, and lined her eyes. Why not? She liked makeup. She had time. She layered concealer and powder, added smoky shadow, then mascara and a nearly black lipstick with a gloss over it.

She rubbed gel into her hair and got dressed. Black jeans, boots, dark T-shirt. Warm for the Mexican heat, but practical. She packed her suitcase, drank a bottle of water, and stepped out the door.

Noa was sitting in the hallway, her back against the wall, holding a steaming cup of coffee between her hands.

Waiting.

The door clicked closed. Jule stepped back against it.

Damn.

She thought she was free, or nearly free. Now she had a fight in front of her.

Noa looked confident; relaxed, even. She remained sitting, with her knees up. Balancing that foam cup. "Imogen Sokoloff?" she said.

Wait. What?

Did Noa think she was Imogen?

Imogen, of course.

Noa had tried to win Jule over with Dickens. And a sick dad. And godforsaken cats. Because she knew all those things would lure *Imogen Sokoloff* into conversation.

"Noa!" Jule said, smiling, returning to the BBC English accent, her back against the door of her room. "Oh, wow, you surprised me. I can't believe you're here right now."

"I want to talk to you about the disappearance of one Julietta West Williams," Noa said. "D'you know a young woman by that name?"

"I beg your pardon?" Jule shifted her handbag so it went across her body and wouldn't easily come off.

"You can cut the accent, Imogen," said Noa, standing up slowly to keep her coffee from spilling. "We have reason to believe you've been using Julietta's passport. The evidence points to you faking your own death in London a couple months ago, after which you transferred your money to her and took over her identity, possibly with Julietta's cooperation. But now no one has seen her for weeks. She's left zero footprint from shortly after the execution of your will until you started using credit cards under her name at the Playa Grande. Does that sound familiar? I wonder if I could have a look at your identification."

Jule needed to think through all this new information, but there was no time. She had to act now.

"I think you must be confusing me with someone else," she said, keeping the BBC accent. "I'm sorry I didn't come to trivia night. Let me get my wallet out and I'm sure we'll get this all sorted right away."

She faked as if to look into her bag, and in two steps, she was on top of Noa. She kicked the coffee up from underneath. It was still hot and it splashed in the detective's face.

Noa's head jerked back, and Jule swung the suitcase hard. It hit Noa in the side of the skull, knocking her to the floor. Jule brought it up again and slammed it down on Noa's shoulder. Again and again and again. Noa hit the floor and scrabbled for Jule's ankle with her left hand while she reached toward her pant leg with the right.

Was the woman armed? Yes. She had something strapped to her leg.

Jule stamped her boot down hard on the bones of Noa's hand. There was a crunching sound and Noa cried out, but her other hand was still trying to grab Jule's ankle, to tip her off balance.

Jule steadied herself against the wall and kicked Noa in the face. As the detective coiled back, bringing both hands up to protect her eyes, Jule yanked the leg of Noa's jeans up.

A gun was strapped to Noa's calf. Jule pulled it off.

She held the gun on Noa and backed away down the hall, dragging her suitcase as she aimed.

When she hit the stairway, Jule turned and ran down it.

Out the back entrance of the inn, she scanned the trash

cans and the cars packed in the back lot. There were bicycles leaning against the back of the building.

No. Jule couldn't take a bike, because she couldn't leave the suitcase.

Farther down the hill, the street opened onto a plaza with a café.

No, that was too obvious.

Jule ran through the inn's parking lot. When she turned the corner of the building, she saw a window into a guest room along the side wall. It was tipped open at the top.

Jule looked into the room.

Empty. The bed was made.

She yanked the screen out of the window and threw it into the room. She pushed her suitcase into the open top—it barely fit—and banged it through the cheap venetian blind. She threw her shoulder bag in and vaulted herself over the windowsill. She scraped her skin going over and landed hard on the floor. Then she shut the window, adjusted the blind, threw her things and the detached window screen into the bathroom, and closed herself in there as well.

The inn was the last place Noa would look for her.

Jule sat on the edge of the bathtub and forced herself to breathe slowly. She unzipped the suitcase and pulled out her red wig. She took off her black T-shirt and put on a white top, then slid the wig onto her head and tucked her hair inside. She closed the suitcase.

She picked up the gun and shoved it down the back waistband of her jeans, like she'd seen people do in the movies.

A couple of minutes later, she heard Noa walk past the

window of the hotel room. The detective was talking on her phone and moving slow. "I know," Noa said. "I underestimated the situation, I know that."

A pause. "It was a lightweight thing, an heiress who ran away, you know?" Noa had stopped walking and was easy to hear. "A silly rich girl on a spree. Evidence so far makes it seem like she and her friend staged a suicide that was gonna let them both live large. The two figured to run off together. They wanted to escape the usual—obsessive ex-boyfriend, controlling parents. The friend thought they were going to share the heiress's money, but the heiress does the double cross. She takes her friend's ID as planned, and then she gets rid of the friend entirely. . . . A contract hit's our best guess, probably in the UK. The friend is now missing, last seen in London back in April. Meanwhile, the heiress, using the friend's details, runs away with all that money and would be living happy, except the obsessive boyfriend can't believe she killed herself, so he keeps hounding the police. Finally, they come to think he's got a point. They look into it, and eventually they find the friend's credit card being used at this Mexican resort."

Another pause while Noa listened. "Come on. A girl like that, a Vassar girl, you don't expect an offensive. No one would. She's barely five feet tall. She wears three-hundred-dollar sneakers. You can't call me out on that."

Another pause, and Noa's voice began to fade as she walked away. "Well, send somebody, because I need medical attention. The kid has my weapon. Yeah, I know, I know. Just send me some local help, *comprende?*"

Forrest had sent detectives. Jule understood it now. He

had never accepted Immie's suicide, had suspected Jule from the get-go, and what had all his vigilant questioning turned up? He'd been told that Imogen had committed fraud to get away from him, and that poor, dead Jule had been nothing but a gullible victim.

Jule left the bathroom, crawled across the floor, and crouched beneath the window to look out. Noa was walking down the hill, clutching her arm and shoulder as she went.

There was a supercabos bus coming down the road. Jule grabbed the suitcase and rolled it into the hall, then stepped out of the inn through a side door. She walked calmly onto the edge of the road and put her arm in the air.

The bus stopped.

She breathed.

Noa did not turn.

Jule stepped into the cab of the bus.

Noa still did not turn.

Jule paid her fare, and the doors of the bus closed. A car pulled up to where Noa stood, cradling her broken hand. The detective flashed ID to the person inside.

The bus pulled away in the opposite direction. Jule sat down on the worn seat nearest the driver.

It would stop anywhere she wanted to get off. That was how the supercabos worked. *"Quiero ir a la esquina de Ortiz y Ejido. ¿Puedes llevarme cerca de allí?"* Jule asked. Ortiz off Ejido—that was where the hotel clerk had told her a guy sold used cars for cash. No questions asked.

The driver nodded.

Jule West Williams leaned forward in her seat.

She had four passports, four driver's licenses, three wigs,

several thousand dollars in cash, and a credit card number belonging to Forrest Smith-Martin that would do for buying plane tickets.

In fact, there were a number of things Jule could do with that Smith-Martin credit card. She *could* pay Forrest back for all the trouble he'd caused her.

It was tempting.

But she probably wouldn't bother. Forrest was nothing to Jule, now that she didn't need to be Imogen Sokoloff any longer.

The last bits of Immie that had been inside her slipped away, like pebbles washed off a shore by a tide going out.

Going forward, Jule would become something else entirely. There would be other bridges to walk across and other dresses to wear. She had changed her accent, had changed her very being.

She could do it again.

Jule took off the jade viper ring, threw it on the floor, and watched as it rolled to the back of the bus. In Culebra, no one looked at identification.

The gun felt hot against her back. She was armed. She had no heart to break.

Like the hero of an action movie, Jule West Williams was the center of the story.

AUTHOR'S NOTE

I was inspired by many, many books and films in the writing of *Genuine Fraud:* Victorian orphan stories, con artist tales, antihero novels, action movies, noir films, superhero comics, tales told backward, stories of class mobility, and books about the lives of ferociously ambitious, unhappy women. The novel I have written feels to me like layer upon layer of references. I cannot possibly name all my influences, but particular debt goes to Patricia Highsmith for *The Talented Mr. Ripley,* to Mark Seal for *The Man in the Rockefeller Suit,* and to Charles Dickens for *Great Expectations.*

ACKNOWLEDGMENTS

Thanks to my early readers for their detailed feedback: Ivy Aukin, Coe Booth, Matt de la Peña, Justine Larbalestier, and Zoey Peresman. Even bigger thanks to Sarah Mlynowski, who read multiple drafts. Photographer Heather Weston created a gorgeous set of images inspired by the novel and added a lot to my understanding of its aesthetic. I'm indebted to Ally Carter, Laura Ruby, Anne Ursu, Robin Wasserman, Scott Westerfeld, Gayle Forman, Melissa Kantor, Bob, Meg Wolitzer, Kate Carr, Libba Bray, and Len Jenkin for support and kibbitzing. My agent, Elizabeth Kaplan, has been a champion; her assistant, Brian McGuffog, a huge help. Thanks to Jane Harris and Emma Matthewson at HotKey and to Eva Mills and Elise Jones at Allen and Unwin for their early enthusiasm. Thanks to Ramona Jenkin for medical expertise. Gratitude to the amazing team at Penguin Random House, including but not limited to John Adamo, Laura Antonacci, Dominique Cimina, Kathleen Dunn, Colleen Fellingham, Anna Gjesteby, Rebecca Gudelis, Christine Labov, Casey Lloyd, Barbara Marcus, Lisa Nadel, Adrienne Waintraub—and in particular to my demanding, patient, and encouraging action-hero editor, Beverly Horowitz. Thanks to my family, near and far, and to Daniel Aukin most of all.

ABOUT THE AUTHOR

e. lockhart wrote the *New York Times* bestseller *We Were Liars,* which is also available in a deluxe edition with new material included. Her other books include *Fly on the Wall, Dramarama, The Disreputable History of Frankie Landau-Banks,* and the Ruby Oliver Quartet: *The Boyfriend List, The Boy Book, The Treasure Map of Boys,* and *Real Live Boyfriends.* Visit her on-line at emilylockhart.com and follow @elockhart on Twitter.

Turn the page for a preview of
E. Lockhart's *New York Times* bestseller
we were liars

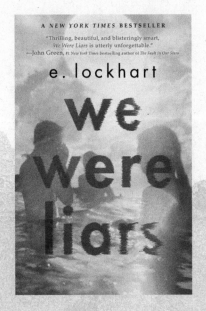

A *NEW YORK TIMES* BESTSELLER

"Thrilling, beautiful, and blisteringly smart,
We Were Liars is utterly unforgettable."
—John Green, #1 *New York Times* bestselling author of *The Fault in Our Stars*

e. lockhart
we were liars

"**THRILLING,** beautiful, and blisteringly smart, *We Were Liars* is
UTTERLY UNFORGETTABLE." —JOHN GREEN, #1 *NEW YORK TIMES*
BESTSELLING AUTHOR OF *THE FAULT IN OUR STARS*

"You're going to want to remember the title. *Liars* details the summers of
a girl who harbors a **DARK SECRET,** and delivers a satisfying, but
SHOCKING twist ending."   —*ENTERTAINMENT WEEKLY*

"An **AMBITIOUS** novel with an engaging voice, a **CLEVER** plot
and some terrific writing."   —*THE NEW YORK TIMES BOOK REVIEW*

"**HAUNTING,** sophisticated . . . a novel so **TWISTY** and well-told
that it will appeal to older readers as well as to adolescents."

—*THE WALL STREET JOURNAL*

1

WELCOME TO THE beautiful Sinclair family.

No one is a criminal.

No one is an addict.

No one is a failure.

The Sinclairs are athletic, tall, and handsome. We are old-money Democrats. Our smiles are wide, our chins square, and our tennis serves aggressive.

It doesn't matter if divorce shreds the muscles of our hearts so that they will hardly beat without a struggle. It doesn't matter if trust-fund money is running out; if credit card bills go unpaid on the kitchen counter. It doesn't matter if there's a cluster of pill bottles on the bedside table.

It doesn't matter if one of us is desperately, desperately in love.

So much

in love

that equally desperate measures

must be taken.

We are Sinclairs.

No one is needy.

No one is wrong.

We live, at least in the summertime, on a private island off the coast of Massachusetts.

Perhaps that is all you need to know.

2

MY FULL NAME is Cadence Sinclair Eastman.

I live in Burlington, Vermont, with Mummy and three dogs.

I am nearly eighteen.

I own a well-used library card and not much else, though it is true I live in a grand house full of expensive, useless objects.

I used to be blond, but now my hair is black.

I used to be strong, but now I am weak.

I used to be pretty, but now I look sick.

It is true I suffer migraines since my accident.

It is true I do not suffer fools.

I like a twist of meaning. You see? *Suffer* migraines. Do not *suffer* fools. The word means almost the same as it did in the previous sentence, but not quite.

Suffer.

You could say it means endure, but that's not exactly right.

MY STORY STARTS before the accident. June of the summer I was fifteen, my father ran off with some woman he loved more than us.

Dad was a middling-successful professor of military history. Back then I adored him. He wore tweed jackets. He was gaunt. He drank milky tea. He was fond of board games and let me win, fond of boats and taught me to kayak, fond of bicycles, books, and art museums.

He was never fond of dogs, and it was a sign of how much he loved my mother that he let our golden retrievers sleep on the sofas and walked them three miles every morning. He was never fond of my grandparents, either, and it was a sign of how much he loved both me and Mummy that he spent every summer in Windemere House on Beechwood Island, writing articles on wars fought long ago and putting on a smile for the relatives at every meal.

That June, summer fifteen, Dad announced he was leaving and departed two days later. He told my mother he wasn't a Sinclair, and couldn't try to be one, any longer. He couldn't smile, couldn't lie, couldn't be part of that beautiful family in those beautiful houses.

Couldn't. Couldn't. Wouldn't.

He had hired moving vans already. He'd rented a house, too. My father put a last suitcase into the backseat of the Mercedes (he was leaving Mummy with only the Saab), and started the engine.

Then he pulled out a handgun and shot me in the chest. I was standing on the lawn and I fell. The bullet hole opened wide and my heart rolled out of my rib cage and down into a flower bed. Blood gushed rhythmically from my open wound,

then from my eyes,

my ears,

my mouth.

It tasted like salt and failure. The bright red shame of being unloved soaked the grass in front of our house, the bricks of the path, the steps to the porch. My heart spasmed among the peonies like a trout.

Mummy snapped. She said to get hold of myself.

Be normal, now, she said. Right now, she said.

Because you are. Because you can be.

Don't cause a scene, she told me. Breathe and sit up.

I did what she asked.

She was all I had left.

Mummy and I tilted our square chins high as Dad drove down the hill. Then we went indoors and trashed the gifts he'd given us: jewelry, clothes, books, anything. In the days that followed, we got rid of the couch and armchairs my parents had bought together. Tossed the wedding china, the silver, the photographs.

We purchased new furniture. Hired a decorator. Placed an order for Tiffany silverware. Spent a day walking through art galleries and bought paintings to cover the empty spaces on our walls.

We asked Granddad's lawyers to secure Mummy's assets.

Then we packed our bags and went to Beechwood Island.

3

PENNY, CARRIE, AND Bess are the daughters of Tipper and Harris Sinclair. Harris came into his money at twenty-one after Harvard and grew the fortune doing business I never bothered to understand. He inherited houses and land. He made intelligent decisions about the stock market. He married Tipper and kept her in the kitchen and the garden. He put her on display in pearls and on sailboats. She seemed to enjoy it.

Granddad's only failure was that he never had a son, but no matter. The Sinclair daughters were sunburnt and blessed. Tall, merry, and rich, those girls were like princesses in a fairy tale. They were known throughout Boston, Harvard Yard, and Martha's Vineyard for their cashmere cardigans and grand parties. They were made for legends. Made for princes and Ivy League schools, ivory statues and majestic houses.

Granddad and Tipper loved the girls so, they couldn't say whom they loved best. First Carrie, then Penny, then Bess, then Carrie again. There were splashy weddings with salmon and harpists, then bright blond grandchildren and funny blond dogs. No one could ever have been prouder of their beautiful American girls than Tipper and Harris were, back then.

They built three new houses on their craggy private island and gave them each a name: Windemere for Penny, Red Gate for Carrie, and Cuddledown for Bess.

I am the eldest Sinclair grandchild. Heiress to the island, the fortune, and the expectations.

Well, probably.

4

ME, JOHNNY, MIRREN, and Gat. Gat, Mirren, Johnny, and me.

The family calls us four the Liars, and probably we deserve it. We are all nearly the same age, and we all have birthdays in the fall. Most years on the island, we've been trouble.

Gat started coming to Beechwood the year we were eight. Summer eight, we called it.

Before that, Mirren, Johnny, and I weren't Liars. We were

nothing but cousins, and Johnny was a pain because he didn't like playing with girls.

Johnny, he is bounce, effort, and snark. Back then he would hang our Barbies by the necks or shoot us with guns made of Lego.

Mirren, she is sugar, curiosity, and rain. Back then she spent long afternoons with Taft and the twins, splashing at the big beach, while I drew pictures on graph paper and read in the hammock on the Clairmont house porch.

Then Gat came to spend the summers with us.

Aunt Carrie's husband left her when she was pregnant with Johnny's brother, Will. I don't know what happened. The family never speaks of it. By summer eight, Will was a baby and Carrie had taken up with Ed already.

This Ed, he was an art dealer and he adored the kids. That was all we'd heard about him when Carrie announced she was bringing him to Beechwood, along with Johnny and the baby.

They were the last to arrive that summer, and most of us were on the dock waiting for the boat to pull in. Granddad lifted me up so I could wave at Johnny, who was wearing an orange life vest and shouting over the prow.

Granny Tipper stood next to us. She turned away from the boat for a moment, reached in her pocket, and brought out a white peppermint. Unwrapped it and tucked it into my mouth.

As she looked back at the boat, Gran's face changed. I squinted to see what she saw.

Carrie stepped off with Will on her hip. He was in a baby's yellow life vest, and was really no more than a shock of white-blond hair sticking up over it. A cheer went up at the sight of him. That vest, which we had all worn as babies. The hair. How wonderful that this little boy we didn't know yet was so obviously a Sinclair.

Johnny leapt off the boat and threw his own vest on the dock. First thing, he ran up to Mirren and kicked her. Then he kicked me. Kicked the twins. Walked over to our grandparents and stood up straight. "Good to see you, Granny and Granddad. I look forward to a happy summer."

Tipper hugged him. "Your mother told you to say that, didn't she?"

"Yes," said Johnny. "And I'm to say, nice to see you again."

"Good boy."

"Can I go now?"

Tipper kissed his freckled cheek. "Go on, then."

Ed followed Johnny, having stopped to help the staff unload the luggage from the motorboat. He was tall and slim. His skin was very dark: Indian heritage, we'd later learn. He wore black-framed glasses and was dressed in dapper city clothes: a linen suit and striped shirt. The pants were wrinkled from traveling.

Granddad set me down.

Granny Tipper's mouth made a straight line. Then she showed all her teeth and went forward.

"You must be Ed. What a lovely surprise."

He shook hands. "Didn't Carrie tell you we were coming?"

"Of course she did."

Ed looked around at our white, white family. Turned to Carrie. "Where's Gat?"

They called for him, and he climbed from the inside of the boat, taking off his life vest, looking down to undo the buckles.

"Mother, Dad," said Carrie, "we brought Ed's nephew to play with Johnny. This is Gat Patil."

Granddad reached out and patted Gat's head. "Hello, young man."

"Hello."

"His father passed on, just this year," explained Carrie. "He and Johnny are the best of friends. It's a big help to Ed's sister if we take him for a few weeks. And, Gat? You'll get to have cookouts and go swimming like we talked about. Okay?"

But Gat didn't answer. He was looking at me.

His nose was dramatic, his mouth sweet. Skin deep brown, hair black and waving. Body wired with energy. Gat seemed spring-loaded. Like he was searching for something. He was contemplation and enthusiasm. Ambition and strong coffee. I could have looked at him forever.

Our eyes locked.

I turned and ran away.

Gat followed. I could hear his feet behind me on the wooden walkways that cross the island.

I kept running. He kept following.

Johnny chased Gat. And Mirren chased Johnny.

The adults remained talking on the dock, circling politely around Ed, cooing over baby Will. The littles did whatever littles do.

We four stopped running at the tiny beach down by Cuddledown House. It's a small stretch of sand with high rocks on either side. No one used it much, back then. The big beach had softer sand and less seaweed.

Mirren took off her shoes and the rest of us followed. We tossed stones into the water. We just existed.

I wrote our names in the sand.

Cadence, Mirren, Johnny, and Gat.

Gat, Johnny, Mirren, and Cadence.

That was the beginning of us.

* * *

JOHNNY BEGGED TO have Gat stay longer.

He got what he wanted.

The next year he begged to have him come for the entire summer.

Gat came.

Johnny was the first grandson. My grandparents almost never said no to Johnny.

5

SUMMER FOURTEEN, GAT and I took out the small motorboat alone. It was just after breakfast. Bess made Mirren play tennis with the twins and Taft. Johnny had started running that year and was doing loops around the perimeter path. Gat found me in the Clairmont kitchen and asked, did I want to take the boat out?

"Not really." I wanted to go back to bed with a book.

"Please?" Gat almost never said please.

"Take it out yourself."

"I can't borrow it," he said. "I don't feel right."

"Of course you can borrow it."

"Not without one of you."

He was being ridiculous. "Where do you want to go?" I asked.

"I just want to get off-island. Sometimes I can't stand it here."

I couldn't imagine, then, what it was he couldn't stand, but I said all right. We motored out to sea in wind jackets and bathing suits. After a bit, Gat cut the engine. We sat eating pistachios and breathing salt air. The sunlight shone on the water.

"Let's go in," I said.

Gat jumped and I followed, but the water was so much colder than off the beach, it snatched our breath. The sun went behind a cloud. We laughed panicky laughs and shouted that it was the stupidest idea to get in the water. What had we been thinking? There were sharks off the coast, everybody knew that.

Don't talk about sharks, God! We scrambled and pushed each other, struggling to be the first one up the ladder at the back of the boat.

After a minute, Gat leaned back and let me go first. "Not because you're a girl but because I'm a good person," he told me.

"Thanks." I stuck out my tongue.

"But when a shark bites my legs off, promise to write a speech about how awesome I was."

"Done," I said. "Gatwick Matthew Patil made a delicious meal."

It seemed hysterically funny to be so cold. We didn't have towels. We huddled together under a fleece blanket we found under the seats, our bare shoulders touching each other. Cold feet, on top of one another.

"This is only so we don't get hypothermia," said Gat. "Don't think I find you pretty or anything."

"I know you don't."

"You're hogging the blanket."

"Sorry."

A pause.

Gat said, "I do find you pretty, Cady. I didn't mean that the way it came out. In fact, when did you get so pretty? It's distracting."

"I look the same as always."

"You changed over the school year. It's putting me off my game."

"You have a game?"

He nodded solemnly.

"That is the dumbest thing I ever heard. What is your game?"

"Nothing penetrates my armor. Hadn't you noticed?"

That made me laugh. "No."

"Damn. I thought it was working."

We changed the subject. Talked about bringing the littles to Edgartown to see a movie in the afternoon, about sharks and whether they really ate people, about *Plants Versus Zombies.*

Then we drove back to the island.

Not long after that, Gat started lending me his books and finding me at the tiny beach in the early evenings. He'd search me out when I was lying on the Windemere lawn with the goldens.

We started walking together on the path that circles the island, Gat in front and me behind. We'd talk about books or invent imaginary worlds. Sometimes we'd end up walking several times around the edge before we got hungry or bored.

Beach roses lined the path, deep pink. Their smell was faint and sweet.

One day I looked at Gat, lying in the Clairmont hammock with a book, and he seemed, well, like he was mine. Like he was my particular person.

I got in the hammock next to him, silently. I took the pen

out of his hand—he always read with a pen—and wrote *Gat* on the back of his left, and *Cadence* on the back of his right.

He took the pen from me. Wrote *Gat* on the back of my left, and *Cadence* on the back of my right.

I am not talking about fate. I don't believe in destiny or soul mates or the supernatural. I just mean we understood each other. All the way.

But we were only fourteen. I had never kissed a boy, though I would kiss a few the next school year, and somehow we didn't label it love.

we were liars

is also available in a deluxe edition with
32 pages of exclusive content, including
notes and poems from Gat to Cadence

HC ISBN 978-1-5247-6458-6

EBK ISBN 978-1-5247-6695-5

Underlined

A Community of Book Nerds & Aspiring Writers!

READ

Get book recommendations, reading lists, YA news

DISCOVER

Take quizzes, watch videos, shop merch, win prizes

CREATE

Write your own stories, enter contests, get inspired

SHARE

Connect with fellow Book Nerds and authors!

GetUnderlined.com • @GetUnderlined

Want a chance to be featured? Use #GetUnderlined on social!

Art used under license from Shutterstock.com

1407